Praise for MAUD CASEY

Drastic

"Casey is a sensitive and courageous chronicler. . . . [These] absolutely soar with illuminating little details that crack everything open and reach for hope." —*Hartford Courant*

"Writing in spare prose with macabre humor and an unerring eye for detail, Casey strips souls bare for our enjoyment, laying neurosis and despair in full view." —*Planet* magazine

"Edgy, thought-provoking, and charged with raw emotion, *Drastic* is an impressive collection from a rich and wonderfully unpredictable talent." —JOHN SEARLES, author of *Boy Still Missing*

"Sad and funny both, Maud Casey's warmhearted, fine stories reach like a pair of outstretched arms for comfort and truth."
  —LILY TUCK, author of
  Limbo, and Other Places I Have Lived: Short Stories

"Like Eudora Welty, Maud Casey aims her considerable art at such nearly unsayable recognitions and has crafted a book that is a treasure trove of jewels to live for—stories beautiful, multifaceted, and fierce with light." —STUART DYBEK, author of *The Coast of Chicago*

"The lives in Maud Casey's perfectly titled new book have attained a drastic shape. Propelled by the hard hungers of love and need and desire, her characters reach out, run away, embrace—and are transformed. Writing with power, beauty, and a searing vision, Maud Casey creates stories that change the world before our eyes."
  —ERIN MCGRAW, author of *Lies of the Saints*

"The characters in *Drastic* struggle to understand their lives in ways we can't help but recognize, in prose that is both quiet and illuminating."

—JASON BROWN, author of *Driving the Heart: And Other Stories*

"In *Drastic*, despair is everywhere, but there is hope, too, in unlikely places—Casey tells these stories with a compassionate voice that would give any one of these people a reason to live."

—MARY KAY ZURAVLEFF, author of *The Frequency of Souls*

"The women [and men] in Maud Casey's sharp, daring stories are too smart to be seduced by consumerism, too wild to be sensible, and just wise enough to escape despair. They find their solace in the broken space between the rules, in the moments love cracks the rock face of the ordinary and rescues them."

—ANN DARBY, author of *The Orphan Game*

"Maud Casey snakes beneath our consciousness, one deft sentence at a time, until she's pried from daily life all that concealed its yearnings. *Drastic* is a wholehearted work of art."

—NICHOLAS WEINSTOCK, author of
As Long As She Needs Me

The Shape of Things to Come
A *New York Times* Notable Book

"Casey is a stand-up philosopher posing the most vexing questions about human existence while satirizing the materialistic ways we find to hold our despair at a distance. . . . Casey shows off her strengths: she's funny and inventive . . . and she empathizes with the least of her characters . . . taking a dazzling narrative dare."

—*New York Times Book Review*

"Maud Casey has written a complex, mature, and compelling novel."

—*Chicago Tribune*

"*The Shape of Things to Come*, Maud Casey's accomplished first novel, takes up with the endearingly subversive Isabelle."   —*Elle*

"Isabelle . . . is like that crazy, charismatic friend you had in high school: You never know what she'll do next, but it's sure to be exciting—and you definitely want to stick around for the ride. . . . Isabelle is so vivacious that even though she's utterly confused about her future, we know it'll turn out just fine."   —*Redbook*

"A startling debut. [Casey's] fresh voice emerges like a song that's bound to be a hit."   —*Virginia Quarterly Review*

"Maud Casey is very good at creating characters who are torn between the strong emotions they experience as members of a family and the internal conflicts they struggle with as they try to break away in order to establish independent identities."

—ANNE BEATTIE, author of *The Doctor's House*

"In *The Shape of Things to Come*, Maud Casey examines the danger inherent in reinvention. [She] deftly writes about the struggle out of the tomb, the restoration of sanity, and the search for small peace."

—MARK RICHARD, author of *The Ice at the Bottom of the World*

"Maud Casey's *Shape of Things to Come* is full of lovely sentences and empathetic characters. Her story is as engaging and scintillating as a story told to you by a best friend."

—DARCEY STEINKE, author of *Jesus Saves*

"Isabelle is a millennial treasure. The journey from child to woman, no matter at what age, is poignant and often funny; Isabelle's is both, in spades."   —ANNE RIVERS SIDDONS, author of *Nora, Nora*

"Maud Casey has the rare ability to continually take her fiction one step further than the reader thought possible—into a region where sentences deliver gifts of wit and wisdom. We should all be grateful she has arrived to cheer and charm us."

—ELIZABETH EVANS, author of *Suicide's Girlfriend*

"Maud Casey's characters may be living in Standardsville, Illinois, but there's nothing standard about their story. *The Shape of Things to Come* is a wonderful account of our need to both invent and reinvent ourselves. A deft and generous book."

—MARGOT LIVESEY, author of *Eva Moves the Furniture*

"A woman on the cusp of becoming is the narrator of Maud Casey's finely observed and moving first novel. The pleasures of *The Shape of Things to Come* are many: the myriad delicacies of Casey's prose, her keen intelligence, and her portrait of an unconventional mother and an adult daughter trying out an intimacy whose boundaries they have never tested."   —ELIZABETH BENEDICT, author of *Almost*

"In this rising wave of new fiction in America, it is, as in the new industries that are its future, young women who are riding the currents to shores that are yet distant and unexplored. Maud Casey is floating at the top, and her novel *The Shape of Things to Come* has hit the beach, shiny and curious."

—DAGOBERTO GILB, author of *Woodcuts of Women*

Carol Cohen

About the Author

MAUD CASEY's stories have been published in *The Threepenny Review, Beloit Fiction Journal, The Georgia Review, Confrontation, Shenandoah, The Gettysburg Review,* and *Prairie Schooner.* She received a Pushcart Prize Special Mention for her story "Dirt." Casey's debut novel, *The Shape of Things to Come,* was a *New York Times* Notable Book of the Year. Casey's new novel, *Genealogy,* will be published in 2005. She lives in Brooklyn, New York.

Also by Maud Casey

The Shape of Things to Come

DRASTIC

stories

MAUD CASEY

Perennial

An Imprint of HarperCollins*Publishers*

"The Arrangement of the Night Office in Summer"
was inspired in part by *The Rule of Saint Benedict*.

"Days at Home" was originally published in *The Georgia Review*, Summer 1997,
volume 51, number 2. It was later expanded into the novel
The Shape of Things to Come (William Morrow, 2001).

"Aspects of Motherhood" also appeared in
Shenandoah, Summer 2002.

A hardcover edition of this book was published in 2002 by William Morrow, an
imprint of HarperCollins Publishers.

HarperCollins books may be purchased for educational, business, or sales promo-
tional use. For information please write: Special Markets Department, Harper-
Collins Publishers Inc., 10 East 53rd Street, New York, NY 10022.

First Perennial edition published 2003.

Designed by Bernard Klein

The Library of Congress has catalogued the hardcover edition as follows:

Casey, Maud.
    Drastic : stories / Maud Casey.—1st ed.
        p. cm.
    Contents: Seaworthy — Trespassing — Rules to live — Days at home —
Dirt — Indulgence — Relief — Talk show lady — Genealogy — Drastic —
Aspects of motherhood — The arrangement of the night office in summer.
    ISBN 0-688-17696-8
    1. United States—Social life and customs—Fiction. I. Title.
PS3553.A79338 D73 2002
813'.6—dc21   2002066030

ISBN 0-06-051255-5 (pbk.)

03   04   05   06   07   ❖/RRD   10   9   8   7   6   5   4   3   2   1

CONTENTS

ACKNOWLEDGMENTS

I am extremely grateful for the inspiration, encouragement, and thoughtful editing I received while writing these stories. It would be impossible to list everyone who helped me in these regards, but I am especially thankful to Jane Barnes, Katie Brandi, Annie Brickhouse, Clare, John, Julia, Nell, and Rosamond Casey, Jeremy Chatzky, Meaghan Dowling, Alex Draper, Jesse Drucker, Elizabeth Evans, Sherry Fairchok, Julia Greenberg, Bob Perry, Timothy Schaffert, Robbie Dale Smith, Lorraine Tobias, Meredith Tucker, the University of Arizona MFA program, and Vermont Studio Center. Finally, my deepest thanks to two extraordinarily gifted friends—my editor, Kelli Martin, and my agent, Alice Tasman—without whom I would be a full-time temp.

Six of these stories were originally published in slightly different form in the following:

Beloit Fiction Journal: "Indulgence"; *Confrontation:* "Talk Show Lady; *The Georgia Review:* "Days at Home"; *The Gettysburg Review:* "Seaworthy"; *Prairie Schooner:* "Trespassing"; *The Threepenny Review:* "Dirt."

DRASTIC

SEAWORTHY

WHEN the sun was still high in the sky, giant Clara, the motel owner, came out of the office. The debarked Dobermans—Dolly and Emmy Lou—trotted after her, rubbing mute, pointed heads against her legs as she limped toward the pool. Her bad leg was the result of a night she got mixed up in an argument with some drunk kids who came to visit nearby Dollywood. In the scuffle she'd been pushed off the balcony onto the concrete terrace, her leg bent underneath her.

Irene, who'd been in the pool all morning and all day yesterday and the day before except for meals, knew all this because she and her father, George—who said Clara was six feet, though secretly Irene thought she was much taller—had already been at the motel three days. George sat nearby in one of the yellow and orange plastic chairs, in the shade of the overhang of the motel balcony, with a magazine he'd bought at the convenience store next door. Irene knew he was only pretending to read because yesterday he'd told her he was reading about faraway places, but when Irene had looked through the magazine later, there were no articles about faraway places. She rubbed her wrists against the perfume sample inserts and put her wrists to her neck the way her mother did. Irene liked to pretend that George was her husband. She hadn't decided yet what would become of her mother if she and her father were married. Myra could be the friend who visited and let Irene borrow her clothes. Before setting off, George had promised Irene that he'd told Myra they were going on this trip, that she'd known for weeks, and even though doubt flickered like the beginning of a fire in her mind, Irene wanted it to be true, wanted it to be this easy to run away with her father, to have him to herself for a little while. Irene worried that she didn't miss Myra, but then put it out of her mind and dove deep into the pool.

Clara squatted by the side of the pool, and the dogs shoved their heads into her lap, snapping their huge white teeth together and apart in barkless motion. Clara's brother, who ran the motel when Clara wasn't there, bought the dogs for protection but soon found he couldn't stand their barking. The dogs preferred Clara to anyone else and were happiest the half of the year she wasn't scuba diving (her leg never bothered her in the water) off the coast of North Carolina. The dogs followed Clara wherever she went.

Irene swam over to hang onto Clara's feet. When she met Clara the first day poolside, she tentatively touched Clara's toes, as if by accident, but Clara took hold of her hands and put them around her ankles. "Hold on and kick," she said. Irene loved this—the way Clara had been casual with her from the start.

"What is your first memory, Irene?" Clara asked. "That's when your life really begins. From when you can remember it."

Irene kicked her feet in the water. She took her time answering because being almost eleven—her birthday was tomorrow—she wanted to tell meaningful stories about her life. Lately she'd been frustrated by how many of her memories weren't even her own. Instead they were stories her parents had told her, passed down like secondhand clothes. So she really considered Clara's question. Irene knew Clara would wait because she was that rare kind of adult—patient.

She tried breathing slowly in and out, the way George had shown her to keep her from hyperventilating the way she did sometimes when she first got home from school all eager breathlessness that her mother was still there, but the sight of giant Clara made her want to do something. She didn't know quite what. She remembered hearing for the first time the secret sound of being underwater, like something magic she wasn't supposed to hear but did. The sand shifted beneath, and there was the occasional sound of a fish rippling water. But then, like the faraway fish, the memory swam away.

"Well," Irene said, "I was three and saw the ocean for the

first time. I ran straight in over my head and kept going."
This was something George had told her, but she could
almost feel herself charging through the water until the
world disappeared. It would have to do for now—*play it by ear*
was George's new motto, the one he'd offered her yesterday
when she asked when they were leaving, a question she asked
more because she didn't want to than anything else. They
were headed for Memphis, for Graceland, but when they
reached Gatlinburg, George announced that it would be fun
if they stopped to take in the local scenery. Irene was happy
to stay for weeks or months. Once her spring break was over,
she'd send for her schoolbooks and do homework when she
wasn't swimming and studying to scuba dive with Clara.

"The water is where I'm really happy," Irene said. She
moved her hand across her stomach to feel the ribbed mater-
ial of her bathing suit stretched across her skin.

"I can tell," Clara said. She pushed gently on Dolly's and
Emmy Lou's rear ends and said, "Sit." The big brown dogs
sat down on either side of Clara, still opening and closing
their mouths as if they were barking, and Irene had an urge
to bark for them. Yesterday Irene had watched as Clara pol-
ished the dogs' teeth with Pearl Drops kept in her pocket.
"You're a natural."

Irene tried to hide her smile. She'd been secretly hoping
that Clara would notice what a good swimmer she'd become
in the past couple of days, that she'd recognize Irene's talent
and take her with her on one of her dives. It was true—Irene
had never felt so happy in her life as when she was in the

water. It felt natural, like a place she was always meant to be. Again a wave of guilt over not missing her mother threatened to drown her. Irene kicked her legs furiously, churning up the water.

"She's going to turn into a fish," George called over, having returned from the motel lounge with his midday cocktail.

"There are worse things," Clara said. Irene was grateful to her for taking her side. She could feel George's eagerness for Clara's attention pushing up against her own, and it made her want to push back.

Irene could imagine that—being a fish. She'd spent some time underwater with her eyes opened, looking at the world distant and quivering above her. She clung to the side of the pool with her fingertips and tilted her head back into the water. When she came up, her hair fit her head like a slick cap.

"Tell me about the fish at the bottom of the ocean," Irene said, looking up at Clara's enormous face. She was the biggest woman Irene had ever seen. She imagined Clara had gills in her broad stomach. "Do fish sleep?" She spoke quickly, her words tripping over each other.

"There are fish that sleep leaning against rocks," Clara said in her unwavering voice, clear and strong like a trumpet. She took Irene's hands and placed them on the pool's edge, then sat down next to them, dangling her legs in the water. Irene readjusted herself so her hands lightly touched Clara's strong thighs.

"There are fish that blow a bubble of mucus around themselves like a canopy bed. Then there are fish like sharks that

sleep with their eyes open and just keep swimming all night."
Clara smiled, and this made Irene want Clara to like her even
more.

"Have you seen fish sleep?" Irene asked, sure that Clara
had seen everything there was to see underwater. Clara's
thick calves moved back and forth in the water like paddles.
Clara didn't seem like the sort of woman who had children,
maybe because the fish needed so much of her attention.
That was one of the other things Irene admired about
Clara—her fish focus.

"Yes," Clara said. "I've seen them sleep." She didn't
explain, and Irene enjoyed the mystery.

"Do you know that if you were to study one cell of a
shark's skin under a microscope, you would see that it was
the exact same shape as a shark's tooth?" Clara let Irene con-
sider this and stood and walked over to retrieve the pool net
leaning against the side of the motel. Clara skimmed fallen
leaves and twigs from the pool's surface. Irene thought this
was a very competent thing to do. She looked over to see
George digging in a big bag of pistachios he'd bought at a
roadside stand, fingers stained red from eating them all day.
She'd tried the pistachio nuts, which sounded so good when
her father cracked them between his teeth, but they didn't
taste as good as they sounded, and her father's red fingers
made Irene sad.

"The exact same shape?" George called over.

"Yes, the exact same shape," Clara said. Irene appreciated
that Clara looked at her when she said this, as if she under-

stood that this was knowledge meant for Irene alone. Irene found a twig and pushed it toward Clara's net.

A map marking the route from their home in Brooklyn to Graceland lay like a crumpled napkin across one arm of George's chair. He'd left it outside the first night, and in the morning, when Irene came down to the pool, she retrieved it from where it had blown into the spindly legs of a patio table, folded it up, and put it under the leg of the chair. George would pull it out and look at it from time to time, and then, at the end of the day, put it back under the chair's leg.

Myra loved maps. She'd made her own map of all the buried bones in Brooklyn, the bones in the recently discovered African-American graveyards and the bones buried under the monument in the park near their apartment dedicated to the prison ship martyrs. "Tortured, without water, sleeping in their own feces," Myra had begun one night as a bedtime story. "Myra," George called from the other room. "What are feces?" Irene asked. "Shit," Myra whispered, giggling. "But it's not funny. The British forced the American prisoners of war to sleep in their own shit." Myra nuzzled her face into Irene's neck. "My little girl. My little girl of living bones." "Myra," George said firmly, standing in the hall outside the door, and Irene knew her mother was in trouble again.

"Are you different from spending most of your life underwater?" Irene asked Clara.

"I'm partially deaf in both ears," Clara said. "From the constant change in pressure." She leaned the pool net against one of the yellow and orange chairs.

Irene considered this. "But are you *different*? Like the way your hurt leg doesn't bother you in the water." She watched carefully as Clara ran a palm over her sun-bleached hair, dry and stiff from so much time spent in ocean water, gathering the loose pieces into a barrette shaped like a claw.

"No, not different." Clara smiled a smile unlike the one she'd offered before. This one said she needed to return to the motel office. Irene was proud she knew Clara's code, thrilled that they could communicate without words. "Altered," Clara said.

Though Irene had never heard the word used in this way before, she knew that Clara meant exactly the way Irene felt when she dove to the bottom of the pool, closed her eyes, and made the difference between the liquid on the inside of her body and the outside go away. She was a saltwater baby again, a natural part of the underwater world.

Irene looked over to George. His magazine lay across his lap, and he wasn't even pretending to read anymore. He stared out at the mountains in the distance. It seemed rare these days that where George looked and what he was thinking went together, so Irene knew he wasn't thinking about the mountains. "Your mother is a beautiful woman," George had said to Irene while looking at Myra one night when they went out to dinner before Myra didn't like to leave the house at night.

"What are you reading about?" Irene yelled, partly to catch his attention and partly because, suddenly, she wanted to catch him in a lie.

Clara looked at George, shielding her eyes with a big hand

to her forehead, as if she were saluting. Irene thought she saw shiny scales sparkle on the part of Clara's stomach exposed by her T-shirt riding up.

"I'm taking a quiz on how to be a better wife," he said. Clara laughed in a girlish way that didn't fit her large, fish self. Her laugh was like the girlish laugh of the waitress in a roadside diner who was sugar sweet to Irene, bending down as if she were an infant instead of the scuba diver in training she would soon become.

"Come swim," Irene said, even though her father never did.

"Don't know how," George said, but Irene had seen him when she was small and just learning to move her body through the water. He used strokes the size of Irene's body, diving under Myra's legs and swimming through, coming up spouting water like a whale.

"God appreciates the truth, you know," Irene said, imitating the silky voice of the Bible lady she and George had heard on the radio the other day in the car.

"Ha, ha!" George shouted, bursting from his chair and startling the dogs. "That's my girl!"

"See you later," Clara said, ducking into the motel office, Dolly and Emmy Lou at her heels.

George sat back down and looked out at the mountains again.

Irene and George had listened to a Bible show—"for fun," George said. "You don't hear this kind of thing on radio stations in New York"—as they crossed from Virginia into Tennessee. Irene thought the Bible lady's southern voice was luxurious, but she didn't say that to George. The lady talked about the difference between lies and the truth and how God appreciates the truth. Even though Irene knew George was listening to the show as a joke, that he didn't believe in God because he relied on the beauty of science to hold him in awe, she couldn't help thinking that she too appreciated the truth. Irene thought there was truth—maybe a kind of truth, not the whole truth and nothing but, but a little bit of truth—in the passages Myra secretly read to her from the Song of Songs, Myra's favorite part of the Bible.

> *For, lo, behold, the winter is past.*
> *The rain is over and it is gone;*
> *The flowers appear on the earth; the time of the singing of the*
> *   birds is come, and the voice of the turtle is heard in our land;*
> *The fig-tree putteth forth her green figs, and the vines with the*
> *   tender grape give a good smell.*
> *Arise, my love, my fair one, and come away.*

Irene saw that these beautiful words went so deep they made Myra cry, but Myra called it weeping, the kind of crying that cleansed you and made you good again.

Irene floated on her back with her ears underneath the surface of the water and said words that felt spoken inside her head. "Sky," she said because she was looking that way. "Irene," and it sounded as if someone else was talking to her. She swam along the bottom, listening past the gurgling of the pool drain to her first memory, the beginning of her life in water.

Irene sat on the bottom of the pool cross-legged. She was training herself to hold her breath as long as the Native Americans whose bones Myra claimed to have found. From under the water all the plastic backs of all of the yellow and orange chairs looked like the colorful plastic flags rippling from strings on the gas station islands where she and George had stopped on their way here. Irene was not surprised when things looked like other things. She had seen George use a coffee table for a seat, a bed for a table, a jacket for a pillow. She had seen Myra use her hand as a broom to sweep crumbs and one of George's shirts as a cape to pretend to fly away out of the prison that was actually their apartment.

When they crossed the border into Tennessee, George had pointed out into the world with his finger, back toward Virginia. "You were born on an island off that coast," he said. Irene was practicing rolling the car window down with her toes, but she listened carefully to this story told all her life. She took the time, though, to admire the way her leg looked, not spread out on the seat but bent gracefully like a woman's.

"Surrounded by water on all sides," her father said, dreamy, like the rest of the ride in the car with Irene dozing off and then waking up in different states. He was still pointing, and the story of the island where she was born meant even more with the eye of a dead dog, legs straight up in the air on the side of the road, staring at Irene. "Oh no," George said. "Poor dog," as if Irene couldn't see for herself. The dog's eye was like the eyes of dead fish she'd seen in towns by water, staring cold but curious, asking a question: *What are you doing alive with me dead on the side of the road?* The stiff, dead dog's eye staring seemed like a sign.

Irene rose quickly to the pool's surface, sputtering water.

"Careful there," her father said.

"I *am* being careful," Irene protested. She hated it when he acted like a parent, when he pretended not to notice how well she took care of herself, causing no trouble.

"This is a sign," Myra had told Irene one day as they stood on the lip of the park. George had told Myra not to go into the park with the monument that housed the prison ship martyrs' dead bones, but there it was, a sign in the form of a chewed dog's bone right at their feet. Irene saw the logic too. "This means we are allowed to enter," Myra said. And they did, walking slowly, swinging their feet in circles—like the metal detectors Irene saw the old men use sometimes—slowly so they could pick up any vibrations from buried bones deep underground. "Even after you die," Myra told her, "your bones vibrate from all the living they've absorbed over the years."

When the sun began to disappear behind the mountains, Irene wrapped a towel turbanlike around her head and walked dripping toward the stairs to the room.

"It's her majesty, the Queen of Sheba," George called down. He'd since moved upstairs to the balcony off their room, where he could put his feet up on a table in the shade and use the bathroom if he needed.

Irene rolled her eyes, but she was glad he was paying

attention, glad that they had each other. She realized then how much he needed her but turned her thoughts quickly instead to the motel magic. While she was swimming, the sheets on the twin beds had been replaced with new ones, the top cover turned down; the glass ashtray where her father discarded his pistachio shells replaced by a new, clean one; the thrown-around clothes stacked in a pile on the chair; and clean-smelling towels hung where the rumpled, pool-soaked ones had been.

When they'd first walked into the motel room so neat and orderly—especially compared to their Brooklyn home piled high with Myra's books on Brooklyn's hidden graveyards and the Bible she hid whenever George came home—Irene couldn't believe it. "I can't believe that this is all ours," she said. "I can't believe they give you this."

"They're not giving it to you," George said, but Irene saw the way George looked at the room, saw that he saw it too, the opportunity for peace. When she saw the Bible on top of the bedside table that separated the two beds, she hid it in the drawer. It had been only recently, after Myra had left her job as a secretary at a hospital—"too many almost-bones"—and in secret, when George was in the city working as many jobs as he could as a copy editor to support them now that Myra was no longer working, that Myra had started reading to Irene from the parts of the Bible that scared Irene because they made Myra red in the face. These parts made her laugh instead of cry, which didn't seem very cleansing to Irene.

His eyes are as the eyes of doves by the rivers of waters, washed
with milk, and fitly set.

His cheeks are sweet as a bed of spices, as sweet flowers: his lips
like lilies, dropping sweet smelling myrrh.

Her hand slipped under her robe to rest over one breast, Myra flushed, and Irene imagined she was talking about George, but then Myra would turn to her as if the words were meant for Irene herself.

We have a little sister, and she hath no breasts: what shall we do
for our sister in the day when she will be spoken for?

"I'm your daughter," Irene would remind Myra, and Myra would stop laughing for a moment to consider this.

After they'd put their bags down, George had tousled Irene's hair and walked out on the balcony to stare at the pool. When Irene walked up beside him, though, she saw he wasn't looking at the pool at all. He stared far out into space, to a place in the sky beyond even the mountains, a place that Irene couldn't locate, not yet visible to her child's eye.

The first night Irene became suddenly shy while undressing, even with George on the porch staring out. There they were, just as she'd sometimes wished, just the two of them without Myra. Irene wondered if she'd made this come true. She shook her head, whipping her face with her hair, shaking out the thought. Had she wished for this so hard that she'd made Myra disappear? But when she asked George the night they left whether she should run back inside to wake Myra up to say good-bye, George assured her that Myra needed to sleep. Myra had wandered the house every night for a week, not sleeping, not eating because she said food crowded her mouth. *Her mother needed her sleep*, Irene told herself the way George had told her. Irene was just following instructions. She was a child, after all. She should do what her father told her.

"Ready for dinner?" George appeared from off the porch like a ghost in a story Myra had read to Irene recently. "Are you talking to yourself, little one?" And Irene realized she'd been standing in her bathing suit, arguing with herself out loud in the mirror.

"Just practicing a play I made up," Irene said. She knew how to make herself seem appropriately childlike. She wished that it were true.

"Maybe you'll perform it for Clara after dinner," George said. "Meet you downstairs, okay?"

"Okay." Irene waited until the door closed behind her father to give herself a solid talking-to in the mirror, one that would show she was different from her mother shaking the dog bone at herself. "I'm telling my bones to stay in my body," she'd told Irene when, the night before Irene and George left on their trip, Irene had woken to find Myra in front of Irene's mirror decorated with pictures of Irene's friends, who no longer came over to the apartment. "Stay in there, bones. Hang onto that flesh. Don't abandon the prison ship. The soldiers are coming to save you." Irene heard them in the hall afterward—George telling Myra she was scaring

Irene, scaring him, scaring her doctor, whom she refused to see like the medicine she refused to take, like the hospital she ran away from because it was full of bones, bones with no flesh, skeletons walking around, bossing her around with their rattling bones as if she couldn't see that all they wanted was to steal her flesh, use it for their own. "Shh," George said, "shh, honey. Come to bed, my sweet girl."

At exactly six o'clock George and Irene sat in their regular booth in the motel restaurant for dinner, as they had for the past two nights. The walls of the restaurant were painted ocean blue, and tiny fish swam through reeds and pink coral. Across the street was a karaoke bar whose marquee read DANCE AND SING ALONE! "That's so sad," Irene said the first night, and then George explained to her that *alone* was meant to be *along*, that someone had made a mistake. Still, the sign made Irene tired, and she made it a point to sit with her back to the window. *Why didn't the owners change the sign? That one letter couldn't be so hard*, Irene thought but never said.

Harry, the waiter who looked a thousand years old, threw his arms wide open when he saw Irene. "The little lady's arrived!" he shouted for no one, since the restaurant was always empty at this hour except for George, Irene, and Harry. Irene smiled as hard as she could so he wouldn't ask her to turn her frown upside down the way he did last night.

"Irene, what a beautiful name," he said, putting his crinkly hand on her back.

"It's a beautiful name—she just doesn't know it yet," George said. Irene rolled her eyes and stuck out her tongue. She knew a lot that George didn't even know she knew. Why did he have to embarrass her, talk about her as if she weren't there, remind people she was a child?

"The usual, coming right up," Harry announced. Irene wondered where he got all his energy.

With one finger George traced an eel on the wall. "Years ago," he said, "I would never have thought that this would be my life, that today I would be here."

"Did you think you'd have me?"

"Of course," he said. "Of course, sweetie," he said as if waking from a dream. "Look, what a surprise!"

Clara walked into the restaurant followed by Dolly and Emmy Lou. The dogs lay down on the floor beside the booth, their heads resting over crossed front paws. Clara slid into the booth on Irene's side, her hair down, the salty sun-air washed out. Irene inhaled the fresh shampoo smell deeply. She could swear that Clara's hair had sliver-thin strands of seaweed mixed in. She reached out and touched it without thinking, and Clara laughed, tickling Irene's nose with the soft ends of her hair.

"You know what my first memory was?" Clara said, looking at Irene. "My first memory, where my life really begins, is pulling into a Memphis hotel that was on fire. My parents were tired of driving, so we waited for the firemen to put it out and then stayed in a room that just missed getting burned." Her voice lapped at Irene's ears like gentle waves.

"You don't really remember all that, do you?" George said. Irene wished that she were the fish that could blow a canopy bed around itself, but she felt more like somebody's forgotten shoes on a beach.

"All right," Clara said. "My parents told me most of that story. But I do remember being held in my mother's arms so that all I could see was the black, charred wood of the burned hotel roof against the blue sky. Now that part is true."

It made sense to Irene that Clara began her life in fire. That's what led her to water. It was another one of Irene's thoughts that never made it into actual words. She felt shy with Clara, the way she did in front of someone who knew true things.

Harry returned to the table and laid out the burgers and a cocktail to replace George's empty glass. "Anything for you, Clara?"

"Just visiting with Irene, Harry," Clara said.

"Gotcha," Harry said. Irene saw him wink.

"Do you sometimes say that you remember everything when actually you remember only the charred wood of the roof against the sky?" George put on the radio Bible lady's southern accent. "Well, my friends, that is a lie. And God appreciates the truth."

Everyone laughed, and George continued, spurred on by the attention. "When Irene's daddy asks her to fill the gas tank while he rests his weary self," he began, "does Irene sometimes say that she has heatstroke when actually she plain well doesn't feel like tending to the damn gas tank?

Well, that is a lie, and you know God appreciates the truth."

Irene didn't think it was funny anymore, especially the way George used her as an example in his joke, as if she were something silly and easily knowable.

George's face was red with the effort of imitation. Irene wished he'd stop. "Do you sometimes," and he had to stop to catch his breath, "find yourself in a place and wonder how you got there?"

Harry and Clara were still laughing and waiting for the end of this lie too, faces expectant like arms outstretched to catch a child, but George shook his head as if he were shaking off the words, the way Irene had shaken off her thoughts earlier. She realized this was a gesture she'd learned from him, and when she looked at his stained-red hands she wanted to tell him to wash them.

"There's a fish called a dorado," Clara said, stepping in, rescuing them all. "Underwater it looks black, but once you reel it in and bring it up on board, the fish turns a greenish-blue."

Irene wondered if it hurt the fish to change color like that and whether it knew it was changing colors. She wondered if the fish knew it would never be the same again.

Harry had disappeared from the table, and suddenly the lights in the restaurant went off, but George and Clara didn't look at all surprised. In fact, George acted as if nothing had happened, smiling a huge smile. Dolly and Emmy Lou clicked their teeth and rose from where they lay, circling each other nervously. Clara put her hand over Irene's. Maybe Irene had blown a canopy around herself and Clara, Irene thought;

maybe the lights hadn't gone out at all. They were in the protective bubble, warm and safe, living their separate fish lives.

"Happy Birthday to you! Happy Birthday to you! Happy Birthday, dear Ire-eeene! Happy Birthday to you!" Their voices were like pins poking at the mucus bubble, popping it open. Harry put the cake, candles blazing, down on the table in the midst of the burger wreckage.

Irene looked at George's face rosy with pride for this party he'd created. "My birthday is tomorrow," she said. She was through looking out for him.

He stared at her the way she'd seen him stare at Myra, as if he wanted her to disappear. "Well, it's almost tomorrow, honey," he finally said. "A few more hours and it's tomorrow. A few more hours after that, it's the next day and so on and so on." Irene saw him look at Harry and Clara to relate to this grown-up phenomenon.

"I know how that works," Irene said, angry at all the things he thought she didn't understand. "I know a lot of things. And one thing I know for sure is today is not my birthday. Today is the wrong day." She looked at Clara, hoping she would understand that they needed to leave together immediately for the coast of North Carolina where Clara could show her the ropes of the scuba diving business and they would spend half their lives underwater, away from the rest of the stupid world on land, but Clara didn't even move to let Irene out of the booth.

"That's a beautiful cake, honey," she said. "Let's eat this one, and we'll have another one tomorrow."

"I need to get out of this booth right now," Irene said. She was tired of being her father's daughter, and that Clara, the beautiful fish giant, would call her honey just like George had was the last straw. Dolly and Emmy Lou stood alert, opening and closing their mouths, as Irene walked out of the restaurant, leaving all of them to each other.

"Just let her go," she heard her father say to Clara, who had started after her. Irene thought about pushing the restaurant door open as hard as she could, giving it a good thwack, but she already knew the power of not slamming doors.

"Harry, can we save this cake for tomorrow?" she heard her father saying.

In the middle of the night, Irene woke where she'd thrown herself on the bed. She heard a soft splash, the splash of a tiny fish, she thought, because she was having the dream where she breathed with giant lungs underwater as she swam with a large school of fish that tickled her with their flicking tails. But there was another, louder splash that was not part of her underwater dream. She walked over to the sliding-glass window and pushed back the curtain. The pool glowed like mercury in the dark, and Clara held George with giant arms as he floated on the water's surface, blowing bubbles into the water. Harry stood at the pool's edge while Emmy Lou and Dolly paced, toenails clicking against the cement and their eyes on Clara. The three of them looked up and saw Irene standing behind the sliding-glass window. They motioned for her to come down.

"She's teaching me to use my lungs to their best capacity," George called up.

Irene did not yell down that she knew he already knew how to swim, that she had seen him hold his breath for what seemed like hours in contests with Myra, who always came up for air too soon. She looked at Clara's long arms—they could still carry her far under the ocean past barnacled rocks, past the fish and seaweed visible from the surface, to water so blue it was black, to a place where there were animals no one had ever seen before.

She looked at George and remembered a yellow afternoon on the island where she was born, Myra watching George cut the still-beating heart out of a tautog and place it in Irene's open palm. This was not a story told to her by her parents, not one she remembered fully except for the tiny boom of a heart in her hand. Irene watched her father with his face in the water. The map, under the leg of the yellow and orange chair, rustled in the night air. In the water, George, like the dorado, was turning color. Under the pool lights he was becoming a fluorescent yellow so bright it was as if he were glowing from the inside out, his insides almost visible in the brightness. Irene slid the glass door open and stepped out onto the balcony, waiting for the tiny booming heart, the heart of her first memory, to tell her the rest of her life.

TRESPASSING

Lucy fingered the strands of the dead man's hair before she sealed the envelope, sticking the prickly ends up her nose to see what the dead man must have smelled like, but the hair smelled mostly like formaldehyde and shampoo.

The program didn't return the ashes of the donor; the cremains were scattered at sea with the cremains of hundreds of other donors. Lucy was supposed to use this word—*cremains*—whenever she spoke to potential donors or their next of kin. Her boss, Mildred, insisted. Mildred was the sort of woman who was always insisting. So far, in the month Lucy'd been at this job, she'd used the word in conversations with cousins, grandsons, granddaughters, husbands, wives, sons, and brothers. "You do understand that we are unable to return the cremains to the family," Lucy would say as earnestly as she could. She practiced saying it to her reflection in the sleeping computer. *Cremains* was a word Lucy imagined had been invented by the same clever ad guy who came up with Craisins, the snack food combination of cranberries and raisins.

"Cremains," Lucy whispered as Mildred gathered her purse and coat on her way out of the office to one of her alleged all-day meetings. Mildred turned quickly, hoping to catch Lucy midwhisper, but she never could. This time Lucy played dumb by neatening a stack of Instructions for the Disposition of Remains forms with concentrated intensity.

"Cremains," again, as Mildred put her hand on the doorknob. Mildred spun around, but Lucy coughed and began to hum like a grade school delinquent.

"I'm very sorry for your loss," Mildred reminded her. Whenever Mildred suspected Lucy of something, she lectured her on etiquette. "You always forget that part when you speak to potential donors. Read it off the cheat sheet if you have to. I know you're a temp, Lucy, but you're a *long-term* temp, and you really should practice good phone manners."

Lucy wasn't very good at any of the primary duties of her job—answering the phone, filing, copying forms like the Vital Statistics sheet, delivering papers to the morgue—but she and Mildred both knew that it would be hard to replace her. There weren't very many people willing to work in such close proximity to the dead, or almost dead. Even Mildred was looking for a transfer. Podiatry or neurosurgery, she'd told Lucy in a rare moment of intimacy that had sliced through the dull hum of the office's fluorescent lights. The way Mildred's face tightened after she revealed this, as if she were willing the confession back into her mouth, Lucy understood not to point out the vagueness of Mildred's desires.

"Got it," Lucy said to Mildred, now waiting at the door for confirmation of her hanging-by-a-thread authority.

"Good," Mildred said. She slammed the door behind her for punctuation. She tried to storm off, but her coat got caught and jerked her back. She opened the door again without looking at Lucy, pulled her coat out, and then stormed off.

Alone in the small, windowless basement office of the university's medical center, Lucy pictured piles of ashes, piles like chimney soot, aboard a barge headed out into the Pacific. A barge like a giant ashtray, which reminded her of the tiny piles of ashes all over her apartment. Since arriving in San Francisco a little over a month ago, Lucy had been living in an apartment with two French girls who needed a third to make the rent. The girls never brushed their hair and were nonchalantly, effortlessly beautiful. They ate only bread and chocolate yet remained mysteriously, aggressively svelte in their American designer jeans. They chain-smoked, ashing in or on anything available—crumb-filled plates, Lucy's potted plant, windowsills. Ash floated constantly in the toilet bowl, unflushed.

Lucy copied Release of Claim forms, sorting them into careful piles. She made copies of the informational packet. There were certain medical conditions that prevented people from donating their bodies to science. Medical students needed to work on "clean" bodies, as Mildred liked to explain over and over again as if it were an incantation, as if by saying this she could ward off hepatitis, HIV, tuberculosis, Creutzfeldt-Jakob disease, whatever that was. Lucy figured she still had a good fifty, sixty years to go in her own body. She appreciated the muscle in her licking tongue, the smell of her arm, an earthy smell that she had, until just the other day, attributed to her cross-country lover until she realized that it was the smell of her own epidermis (Lucy liked to use medical terms on the job). She imagined small fossils of her life lodged in the sedimentary layers of her epidermis, secretly and forever, tiny gifts to herself.

Lucy heard Brenda's mail cart in the hallway. She quickly ducked beneath her desk, fixed her face in the maniacal way she practiced whenever she went to the bathroom, and popped up when Brenda opened the door. Brenda, who hadn't thought this was funny the first five times, barely flinched. Without a word, she threw the mail on the chair beside the door and resignedly rolled her cart away.

Since she'd started working at the whole-body donation program, the French girls' tiny piles of ash had started to creep Lucy out. This morning before work, she had asked them to smoke outside the apartment.

"But zese new American laws," the thinner, dirtier, slightly more beautiful one protested, suddenly bursting into English, having barely uttered a non-French word since Lucy met her. "If we cannot smoke een our own houze, where would we zmoke?"

"How about on zee ztoop?" Lucy asked. Neither of them spoke to her for the rest of the morning, though the slightly less beautiful one had cracked a window and angrily puffed her smoke outside. "Ça suffit?" she'd said to her friend, who rolled her eyes.

Ryan, the removal service driver, stuck his head in the door. "What goes on, my friend?"

Lucy never heard him coming, but Ryan didn't inspire her to spring like a maniacal jack-in-the-box from underneath her desk. Ryan was the first adult who had treated Lucy like an equal. He was handsome in a craggy, been-around-the-block kind of way and older than Lucy, older even than the twenty-eight-year-old cross-country lover—a word Lucy liked to say out loud in the bathroom after she practiced her maniacal face. "Lover," Lucy would say dramatically, pursing her lips and pouting a little. Lucy suspected Ryan might even be in his early forties.

"You've still got your scarf on," Lucy said, touching her own throat. Ryan pulled one end of the flowery scarf he wrapped Audrey Hepburn–like around his head whenever he drove. It swirled around his neck as he pulled; then he stuffed it deep into the pocket of his gray coveralls. Ryan wore women's clothes when he moved bodies, a hangover from his delinquent days before he found his calling in transporting cadavers. He'd accumulated several DWIs, had his license revoked, and started dressing in drag to evade the cops. He grew to like the way the skirts left room for a breeze, the way the scarves billowed silkily against his face, the way the big movie starlet sunglasses hid his face. He slipped the coveralls on and off easily over his outfits before he entered a home or the medical center.

"That's a lot of work for a little silk," Lucy said.

"It's a ritual," he said, shrugging. "Something to keep me out of trouble. Back in a minute—I left my smokes in the morgue."

Lucy could understand a ritual like that. Sometimes she gripped the edges of her desk in an effort to keep herself from vanishing into thin air. Please stop. Lucy felt the slip begin. She felt herself sliding out of normal time. Minutes flying, whizzing, by her. She was nauseated from all the flying and whizzing. She clung to the arms of her chair, waiting for it to pass.

The same thing had happened the morning after she and the cross-country lover spent the night in the van outside a rest stop. After a dinner of potato chips and whiskey, she woke up in the morning to the sounds of a little girl learning to ride a bike in the parking area. Her father ran behind her. "Keep it up! Keep it up!" he cried. "I can't, I can't," she said, but she did. Lucy shook her cross-country lover awake to explain how waking up in the same clothes she'd worn yes-terday with whiskey on her breath, smelling of drunken, halfhearted sex on the side of the road to the sounds of her own lost innocence made her feel like something was rotting inside her, like her heart was black and shrinking. She needed him to understand that. Could he understand that?

"You're young, you'll get over it," he said. As he liked to remind her, twenty-one and just out of college was light-years away from twenty-eight. "You're hungover. You just need a greasy meal," he said.

Ryan stuck his head back in the door. "Gotta run. I'm late. I stayed to help clean up again. This one was a real mess—a recluse with fifteen cats." He aspired to one day running his own cleanup company, providing maid services for the families of the recently deceased, cleaning up the area where the person died so the family didn't have to. Changing sheets, sweeping up. He had the perfect French maid's outfit at home.

"But before I go—Mrs. Sally Calhoun," Ryan said, reading the name off a sheet of paper.

"Sally Calhoun," Lucy repeated, thinking back over the calls she'd taken. "Sally, Sally, Sally. Calhoun, Calhoun, Calhoun." In an effort to help Lucy feel more connected to her job, Ryan told her the names of the bodies he transported in case they ever matched a person whose intake she'd done. So far, they hadn't.

"Nope," Lucy said.

"Hey, you might finally get your earthquake," Ryan said.

"Don't tease me, Ryan." Lucy longed for her first earthquake, the big one, the quake that would come and shake her life, sievelike, until the secrets dislodged from the sedimentary layers of her epidermis, revealing themselves to her.

"Last night on the news, there was an earthquake that stretched from San Diego to Santa Barbara. Six point three. Humboldt started shaking today." He wagged a scolding finger at her.

"I'll believe it when I see it."

"It's not something you see," Ryan said. "It's like death."

"Yeah, whatever, you're not going to give me that lecture again, are you?" Ryan often expounded on his theory of existence: if humans could really see forward to their own deaths, they'd never move forward, a balking mule of a species.

Lucy did her best bray.

"I'm out of here." Ryan winked and was gone.

Lucy felt the earthquake moving toward her. It would knock a few sizable pictures off the wall and send a quiver so hard up her thigh she would have multiple orgasms. But still, the feeling that her organs were decaying slowly, that she was dying, wouldn't lift. This morning she'd woken up convinced again that she had AIDS. The cross-country lover had injected heroin years ago. He'd slept with bedloads of women and a handful of men. "Have you been tested?" she asked him one morning, shaking him awake. She was always shaking him awake.

"Several times," he'd assured her without opening his eyes. So maybe she had cancer. She could feel its slow, deliberate movement through her system. "What does cancer look like?" she asked, putting her hand on his arm. "I don't believe this," he said, wrapping the lumpy motel pillow around his head and turning away from her.

"Maybe it's all the fast food," he suggested when Lucy burst into tears outside a Jack-in-the-Box. "Too much grease."

They bought fruit in a grocery store, lingering in the spray that followed a thunderclap in the fruit and vegetable aisle. Lucy looked around at all the other people pushing shopping carts, somehow leading normal lives, deciding between whole milk or 2%, unperturbed.

"We're trespassing," Lucy said. Maybe she had a disease that no one had ever heard of, something so complex and insidious that doctors would only be able to find it after she died. "Will you make sure someone does an autopsy on me when I die?"

"Let's get the fucking fruit and get out of here," he said.

"We're homeless," she said. "Transients, nomads." She knew she was being melodramatic. She wanted him to scream at her, give her something to work with.

"You're a nut," he said, drawing her to him. She'd wanted to punch him.

Her first day on the job, Lucy had been quick to make excuses. "I got this job through a temp agency," she told Ryan before he even asked. "You know, it's the kind of thing you talk about later—*that crazy job you had.*" The temp counselor had given it the hard sell—a good job, benefits (unheard of!), but Lucy didn't need convincing. The job was exactly right, the giant question mark at the end of the sentence that was the cross-country death march, an opportunity to look her deepest fear in its cold blue face.

"It's an experience on the way to something else," Lucy continued to explain when Ryan didn't respond. She thought she was being deep in a shallow kind of way. She assumed he'd agree with her, that he felt the same way about working for a corpse removal service.

"An experience on the way to what?" Ryan asked. He wasn't smiling, and Lucy blushed so deeply her hairline burned with the spreading heat.

But Ryan was serious. He wasn't trying to embarrass her; he was genuinely curious.

"I don't know," Lucy confessed.

"It sounds melodramatic, but handling the dead is my destiny," Ryan said.

Lucy wished she could take back her attempt at cynicism and cleverness now that she knew melodrama was allowed.

"I wasted a lot of time," Ryan said. "Now, when I take someone's body from their home to the place where they'll serve science, I feel like I'm doing something useful, something real."

"Yeah," Lucy had said, wishing she could say more.

When Lucy met the cross-country lover, she'd been ready for reality herself. She'd barely made it through college. She couldn't figure out why she was there in the first place. She skipped most of her classes (picked at random from the enor-

mous course catalog—"Nuclear War" and "TV and the Evo-
lution of the Postmodern Family: *Happy Days* to *Once and
Again*"). She was wowed by the possibilities of living on her
own. She learned to flirt and have opinions. She created a lit-
tle business out of making fake ID for freshmen, earned
enough money for the cross-country trip so her parents
wouldn't hassle her. She had planned to drive alone. The
cross-country lover was a bonus.

She'd met him when she went to see a play at the commu-
nity theater. It was a play written by a local author about ter-
rorists who formed a ballet troupe as a front for the
terrorism. Over the course of the play, they learned to love to
dance. The cross-country lover played the tough, wary ter-
rorist who was the last to learn to love ballet.

He and Lucy went for drinks after the show. She'd compli-
mented him on his performance.

"For that, the girl deserves a drink," he said, still wearing
his stage makeup.

"How could I possibly refuse?" Lucy took his arm. He
could be a relationship on the way to other relationships, a
relationship that might teach her valuable lessons.

"The director said I needed to be tougher, more of a ter-
rorist, before I give in to the life of a ballerina," he said, half
laughing. A relationship that would teach her, but still she
had wanted him to worship her just a little, to suggest
impossible things. "I'm terrorist enough, don't you think?"
he said. "How much terrorist does this guy need?"

Come live with me and bear my children! he would plead. *No way*, she'd say, and it would drive him crazy with love.

Lucy's face too would someday be tough and blue, dizzy with formaldehyde, but as Ryan often pointed out, Lucy didn't really know that now. She knew she would be dead the same way she knew she might be married one day or have children. She knew it the same way she knew she might someday have a permanent job, which was to say it wasn't something she could imagine at all.

Lucy decided to stretch her legs. She wandered toward the morgue, walking as slowly as possible to eat up the minutes on the clock, reading all the posters on the bulletin boards along the way—a brown bag lunch on intestinal disorders, an appeal from administrators to the doctors to practice professional behavior in all areas of the hospital, no discussing patients in the elevators (*We're a nation of litigators!* someone had written very lightly in pencil).

At a rest stop in the wide open heat and big sky of west Texas, a toothless guy who'd pitched a tent near the bathrooms tried to pick Lucy up. The cross-country lover interfered. "Hey, man," the toothless guy protested. "This is America. I've got rights." Lucy laughed for hours in the car about this. She took it up as her motto for wanting anything unreasonable—the window up or down, the radio more loud or less loud, driving faster or slower. "Hey, man, this is America. I've got rights!" She said it whenever possible, trying to integrate it into the conversation of their relationship. She wanted it to be their private joke, but it never took.

"Why do you keep saying that?" the cross-country lover finally said somewhere in the endless desert of Nevada. "It's not funny."

When Lucy finally reached the morgue, the door to the embalming room was the tiniest bit ajar. She stood at such an angle that she could see—like watching a horror movie through her fingers—the top of a skull and Hank and Frank (his name was Fred, but it was funnier to call him Frank), the embalmers, maneuvering their way around the body. The movement of their arms suggested tubes and the draining of blood.

Pinned against the wall, looking at the top of the man's head without the man inside, Lucy thought, *This is just a body*. Just the vehicle for whoever that was lying there on the table like food, and now that whoever is gone. Gone somewhere else. This man had offered his shell to feed science, to feed the world, food for mankind.

In Arizona Lucy had bought a broad-rimmed hat to protect her fair skin. She'd hoped that the cross-country lover would buy the hat as a surprise, but when it became clear that he had no surprises in him, she bought it for herself. They stopped on the side of the road to wander through the saguaro cactus Lucy had only seen pictures of in travel magazines.

"They're at least one hundred years old," the cross-country lover said. Lucy ignored him, bored with his knowledge. The sun filled the whole sky. The arms of the saguaros were like humans gesticulating and Lucy stood next to one, her arms held up in imitation. "Who? Me?" she asked, shrugging like a cactus, but the cross-country lover was already heading back to the truck. Lucy stumbled after him, faint with heat, and tripped over what looked like giant ribs made of wood. The cross-country lover was already behind the wheel. "Hey," she cried. She stayed on the ground by the wooden ribs. When he saw her, she was pleased to see him jump out of the van with alarm and run back to her.

"What is this?" she said, running her hand along the smooth wood, when he reached her.

"Saguaro ribs," he said, annoyed that she was uninjured. "Their skeletons are made of wood. You're covered with dust, Lucy."

Lucy scrutinized the sleek wood under her hand. This was all that was left of one of these great giants. She had expected something green, or soft, something to show it was once alive.

Now Lucy stared at the tufty skull of the man on the embalming table, imagining his blood running thick through anonymous tubes. Worse still, his lifeless hands. Hands were the first thing you touched when you met a person. Here, they hung limp with unintentional gesture. That his hands didn't mean anything anymore disturbed Lucy the most. She imagined the medical students cutting into the hundreds of bones in the man's frozen hands like marzipan.

Lucy slipped into the women's rest room to splash cold water on her face. She stared at herself in the mirror, trying to separate herself from her body, like meat from the bone, until she began to look pale. She looked deep into her own eyes. Where was she in there?

She strode down the hall, back toward the office, under the insectlike buzz of the fluorescent lights. The cross-country lover had been a runway model. For a *very, very* short time, for *money*, he'd assured her over those initial drinks. This was before he began his full-fledged career as an actor.

"Community theater is considered full-fledged?" Lucy asked as he motioned for the check.

"Funny, really funny," he'd said, because in the beginning these kinds of questions were what he'd loved about her. An hour later they were back in the apartment she shared with three other girls. It was spring, a few days before graduation, and there were packed boxes everywhere ready for cities bigger and more promising than the college town. She and the cross-country lover wove their way through the maze of boxes on their way to Lucy's bedroom, where they shut the door and tore at each other's clothes until they were completely naked.

"I want to steal your body," he'd said to Lucy, running his hand territorally over her hip.

"Why would you want to do that when I'll give it to you for free," she said, taking his hand and placing it between her legs. It amazed her how easily she spoke these words. She almost laughed out loud but instead channeled this energy into a seductive smile. She was a much better actor than he was. But what had he taken from her? What had they taken from each other—tasting each other, little bites on the verge of cannibalism. They probably still had traces of each other under their nails, in their throats, in their genitals. They had each stolen something. Lucy hoped that he noticed something gone from him too.

Back in the office Lucy doodled on her desk calendar—little faces with enormous eyes and wild hair. She'd thrown things at him in hotel rooms when they argued—shoes, TV remotes, maps—so that later he would remember her as the kind of girl who threw things during arguments, the "wild" girl in his past that his future girlfriends, the legitimate ones, would hate to hear about.

She put an amputated rubber hand that wiggled its fingers in one of the file drawers for Mildred to discover later. She'd found it half price in a magician's shop in Chinatown. Lucy imagined her screaming, "It's those pranksters from the morgue!" Mildred would send the crisp papers of the dead flying everywhere with her flailing arms.

She put her head down on her desk and forced herself to imagine the death of the cross-country lover. It wasn't hard. She'd had a lot of practice. She'd started rehearsing for his death as they drove across the country, her head propped against the rattle of the van window. She imagined a car accident in which his limbs were flung like tree branches, his head like a bowling ball through the windshield. She conjured farm machinery gone wild, threshing him like a sheaf of wheat. Now she allowed herself to imagine him smothered to death in a collapsed snow cave, his dog sled, pulled by dogs who never liked him, fleeing across the tundra without him.

When the phone rang, Lucy lifted her head from the desk and wiped the drool from the corner of her mouth.

I'm very sorry for your loss," Lucy said.

"I'm calling about my wife," said the man. There was a pause, and then he added, "She's dead."

"What is your wife's name, sir?" Instead of rolling herself over in the chair as she usually did, she got up and walked to the potential donor files.

"Her name is Dora. Dora Moore."

Lucy felt so tired. Last night she'd dreamed of endless pastures and vast oceans, landscapes in which she looked for the cross-country lover, but even in her dreams she knew it wasn't him that she was looking for. She searched with the tantalizing taste of salt and earth on her tongue.

"I'm so sorry, Mr. Moore," Lucy said, but she meant "Rescue me."

"She's still wearing the chapstick that I applied before she died, minutes before. She kept saying, 'Lips,' and for the longest time I didn't know what she meant, but then I understood. She even moved her mouth to accommodate the motion while I put it on."

Lucy put her hand on her knee to stop the bouncing, but it was not her knee that bounced. The medical center itself rolled with the rhythm of a loping horse.

"It's an earthquake," Mr. Moore said. "Maybe this house will crumble into dust."

Lucy felt a watery dizziness, and for a second she thought she might be dying, really dying, too.

"I'm sorry, I didn't mean that. Did I mention that Dora is very clean? I bathed her last night after we watched the news. Why we were watching the news as if anything to do with this world would ever have anything to do with us again I don't know."

Lucy wrote down "very clean," even though there was no cleanliness category on the Vital Statistics sheet.

"Mr. Moore, do you feel that shaking?" asked Lucy. She thought of all the bodies in the morgue, their blue fingers trembling, slipping out from under their sheets, no one to put them back. Her knee was really shaking now.

"It's stopped."

"Mr. Moore?" said Lucy.

"Yes," said Mr. Moore. "Yes," he said again.

"It felt like we were still moving," said Lucy. And really, she thought that they were. Rushing forward, faster and faster, spinning into infinity. With her eyes shut, the blackness inside was the blackness outside, her body a meager border. Lucy touched the multicolored scarf around her neck. Knotted loosely at her throat, the chiffon brushed her collarbone. This was the scarf that she used to hide from the sun in the Southwest, the fabric breaking up the Texas sun into flecks of color like a sheltering kaleidoscope.

"There's a raspberry birthmark on her chest," Mr. Moore said. "I'd like you to write that down."

This is the cowlick, thought Lucy, touching the swerve in

her hairline. Licked by cows, the cross-country lover had said.

"My skin smells like Dora."

Lucy was afraid she was somehow responsible for this first earthquake and even more afraid she had nothing to do with it at all. Lucy listened to the gentle sucking sound of Mr. Moore's lips brushing against the mouthpiece. She could hear his terror, and felt her life continue to rush forward, crashing through the dense brush, cutting a clear path to her blue and dizzy face.

"It's stopped," Mr. Moore said again.

"I'm sending someone right away," Lucy said. "You can stay on the line. Stay here on the line."

She paged Ryan, cradling the phone between her shoulder and her cheek.

"We'll wait together," she said.

"Yes," Mr. Moore said.

With Mr. Moore's breath in her ear, Lucy planned her evening—the ride home on the bus, the large chocolate bar she would buy at the corner deli for dinner, the way she would eat it slowly, square by square, letting each square melt on her tongue, not ever biting. She'd apologize to the Frenchies, bum one of their cigarettes, and sit on the stoop listening to the cars go by, the burned-coffee-and-orange-peel smell from the café next door mixing with her cigarette smoke. She would tap the long ash of her cigarette into the air and let it float away as she waited for the relief of boredom.

FROM the shelter lounge, a few days before Christmas, we watch the hard rain flood the playground sandbox. Twice-abandoned toy dump trucks drift over the weather-treated hemlock-board sides. It is a relief to see it flooded—this bizarre thing donated by someone who wanted it out of their yard. A sandbox in a desert town is like a pool in the middle of the ocean. What's the point? I crowd my mind with these kinds of questions.

The rain pounding the dry, cracked earth is a reminder of one pure element of my past, something forgotten, then suddenly remembered now that I no longer live in a world of knowing where the silverware is or the feel of the key in the lock of my own front door. Here in the shelter lounge, we are anyone anyplace, three girls at a slumber party—Mary on the couch doing her nails, me on the phone, Lindy pacing the circumference of the room until she can't stand it any longer because she always feels the need to be doing anything other than what she is doing. She sneaks off to the kitchen for late-night snacks.

I pick numbers randomly from the phone book to postpone my nightly call to Jonathan. This time the woman who answers says "Hello" three times and then waits, playing phone chicken. "Pervert," she says. Before she hangs up, I hear the scrape and clatter of forks and knives against plates, a family eating dinner in the background.

I focus on the rare torrent of rain outside to avoid nostalgia for something that never existed. Dusty red and spare, this unfamiliar landscape is what the moment just before the end of the world will look like. I slept most of the way on the bus ride that lasted days or minutes from my home in the middle of the country, waking up in time to see the pastel stucco houses of the Southwest hunkered down close to the ground, futilely ducking the rays of the big red sun. Saguaros loomed on the side of the road, giant and slightly awkward in their hugeness like freak show tall men. Walking from the bus station to the shelter's confidential location (known only to the people in the apartment complex across the street, the clerks at the Circle K on the corner, and all the bikers who frequent the biker bar down the block and then ride out into the world at large), I passed date palms and aloe vera plants growing impossibly out of dry earth. Outside a faded yellow one-story house lay a rusty car, flipped over and filled with dirt, flowers growing out of its smashed windows.

Which leads me back to Jonathan, so I consider swamp coolers, the strange contraptions specific to this dry climate, their wet cloth pads hanging down so the thin breeze can blow through. What do swamp coolers have to do with swamps? There's nothing swampish about this place.

Like most of the women, I am not from here, though being white I am more from here than the Indian women from reservations, which hover dilapidated and desolate at the edges of the city like guests never invited in, or the Mexican women from the other side of the border. We are all strangers to this place run by helpful white women who provide us with clean sheets and towels and help us to locate ourselves in the slivers of the Power and Control pie chart—economic abuse, sexual abuse, verbal abuse, pushing, hitting, scratching, hair-pulling, knifing and/or other weapon-related violence. The counselors' conversational Spanish is no match for the clicking rhythms spoken by my neighbor Joan, the Tohono O'odham woman who lives in the room next to mine with her ten-year-old daughter whose head is dented from the time her father threw her down the stairs when she was two. The counselors go home at night, except the one who sleeps over, who is especially proud of her ability to pronounce the ah-ah-DOM in Tohono O'odham.

I pick a number from the Cs with my eyes closed and dial carefully. It rings only once. "Why don't you just fuck off?" a crying girl answers midsob. She was expecting someone else, and I apologize. "Who is this?" she asks hopefully. I hang up because I don't want to disappoint her.

"He hung up on you," Mary says, an accusation. She's sure I'm calling Jonathan. She doesn't really care whether I call him or not—she just wants to know everything. I don't even bother denying it because it isn't worth squashing the pleasure Mary takes in thinking that she's right. She lies back, taking up the whole couch where she's been cutting her toenails all evening, the ragged half-moon parings falling onto the thin brown carpet that doesn't reach the edges of the room.

"I'm going to have to vacuum that tomorrow, you know," I remind her. My name is next to Lounge Duty on the chart in the office.

"Fuck chores," she says. "I had enough of that at home. It's like being abused all over again around here." She likes to talk tough to remind us that she comes from tough-talking, working-class New England stock, raised in a town famous for being the home of a woman who murdered her parents with an ax for no apparent reason. She's also in a particularly bad mood because she got into a fight with her counselor this afternoon. The counselor said she saw her hanging out at the biker bar up the street where Mary's new boyfriend spends most nights drinking and playing pool and waiting for Mary. She's spent all afternoon painting and repainting her nails. Now she twists open a bottle of nail polish called Wicked, procured from the makeup closet. The smell is harsh and medicinal.

I reach in the pocket of too-big borrowed pants, all they had in the lounge closet, and discover a quarter. I dig it out and hold it in my hand, remembering the way—before he forbade me to leave the house without him two weeks ago—Jonathan slipped quarters still hot from his clenched hand into mine as if I were a slot machine that might someday give. He liked me to call him from wherever I was going once I'd arrived. Once, he had me put the guy at the gas station on the phone. "She's right here," he told my husband cheerfully and then nodded, laughing. "Sure will. My wife forgets to change the oil, I can't tell you how many times." When he hung up, he smiled at me. "Women," he said, shaking his head.

After Jonathan asked me to quit my job, he called from work on the half hour to make sure I didn't leave the house. The first thing I did when I got to the shelter a week ago was to see how it felt to be on his end of the line. He picked up the phone and said, "Eliza," in a sad echo of a voice that made me want to get back on the bus and go home to him. He sometimes looked at me so hard it was as if I were the only thing in the world that he wanted. If he'd stared me into dust, I would have been grateful.

I dial his number, my old number, and the phone just rings and rings. My heart races—whenever he's not there, I'm sure he's killed himself, but as the counselors around here like to say, I'm projecting. Whenever he is home, I listen to him breathe for a while and then hang up.

"So is someone going to do something about this tree?"

Mary asks, waving her knife. Impatience is Mary's natural tone of voice. In the corner of the lounge, the trashbag filled with ornaments wrapped in paper towels sits next to the artificial tree, which still doesn't have its top put on. The ornaments are mostly glass Christmas balls, green and red, with a few handmade ornaments like the round, smooth, cross-cut piece of wood with MERRY CHRISTMAS MOM, LOVE, PETE '99 painted in alternating blue and purple letters. None of us know who Pete is, and no one hazards a guess because it is an unspoken rule that the immediacy of life here does not allow for questions that travel backward.

Lindy walks into the lounge like the ringmaster at a circus, capturing our attention with the possibilities of what she might do next. Last night she showed us how to shake quarters out of the soda machine, rocking it with hands braced on either side of its frame as if she were reprimanding it. She throws a shrink-wrapped cupcake at Mary and a bag of chips at me.

"Hey, watch the nails," Mary says, brushing the cupcake off the couch as if it were an insect.

"What?" I ask. "No dip?"

"What are *you* going to do about the tree?" Lindy asks, looking at Mary. Mary's voice has a tendency to carry throughout the shelter, but even if it didn't, Lindy hears everything. It's a sense she fine-tuned over the years with her on-again, off-again cop boyfriend who works for the border patrol in Nogales.

"Yeah, right," Mary says. "Merry fucking Christmas."

"What happened with the police this afternoon?" I ask Lindy. Lindy was caught shoplifting earlier today—a container of dental floss she could have gotten from the shelter.

"Wouldn't you know I'd get caught stealing something useful," Lindy says. "He said he'd go easy on me because my life was such a mess. I think he was just disappointed to find out I'm legal. I know my boyfriend was." Lindy's half Mexican, and her boyfriend liked to threaten her with deporting her mother, originally from Hermosillo and now living in California. Lindy's father, who abandoned the family when Lindy was born, is white, born and raised in Iowa, like my parents. My own parents are both dead of natural causes, having lived substantial lives. Their deaths were shocking and shockingly unremarkable.

Our Iowa roots are all Lindy and I have in common, but here, where no one wants to see the thing they have most in common, that is a lot. The distinct groups of women in the shelter only mix in the evening, the time of day when fear hangs most palpably in the air. During dinner we all gather around one table to marvel at each other's tolerance or lack thereof of various spices, and then everyone drifts apart. Usually the Mexican women make their way to the picnic bench in the center of the courtyard; the Indian women gather around the benches near the sandbox; and the white women hang out in the lounge. Lindy, though, is a wild card. She calls her own shots. In here, she goes wherever she likes and no one says anything.

She is my only true friend precisely because of the way

she asks Mary this question about the tree, bold so that she gets what she wants but with a sense of humor so that she can always say she was just kidding and take it back. She's learned how to cover herself. I recognized this quality in her immediately and approached her with tentative determination, letting her know my intentions without seeming desperate. Neediness here is like a disease; no one wants to catch it.

At home, my two friends from my old job stopped calling. I was a receptionist at an all-women's health spa despite my half-finished master's in English that Jonathan nipped in the bud after a year and a half because it made him feel abandoned when I got lost in a book. "What are you escaping from?" he asked. It was easier to just not do it when he was around, and after a while he was around all the time, even when he wasn't.

"Look what we have here, a new box of donations," Lindy says, opening the donation closet next to the washer and dryer. She holds up a kerosene lantern. "In case we decide to join the snow women."

Mary looks up from her toes. "Don't start with that again, Lindy. I'm serious, it gives me the creeps."

At dinner my second night here, Lindy told everyone a story about the women who burrow deep holes in the snow to keep warm when their husbands lock them out. She learned about these women from a resident in a shelter in Colorado where Lindy stayed when she was on the run the first time.

Lindy said these women dig snow caves with their bare hands. There's a maze of underground snow tunnels, she said, and a network of women crawling on all fours, digging with chapped hands. They gather occasionally to light candles and warm their hands so that they can continue to burrow.

"Yeah, yeah," Mary said. "We all got problems." The other women, used to being invisible, had slipped away as Lindy was still talking.

"That's exactly what I'm talking about," she said to Mary.

"I like stories," I said. "Stories are the best part."

"The best part of what?" Lindy asked.

"Of everything," I said.

"Where did you say you were from?" Lindy asked like she thought I was strange, but I knew by then she never asked questions for no reason. After the dishes were done, we sat silently on a neutral bench outside the office, underneath a vast, starry sky, each thinking her own thoughts in the pleasure of each other's company. After a while I told her my parents were from Iowa and she told me her father was also from Iowa, and we considered that coincidence in an intimate kind of silence until a counselor came and told us it was time for us to go to our rooms.

Each item she finds in the lounge closet, Lindy holds up to us for inspection. There's a barely inflated volleyball, bungee cords, heart- and flower-shaped cookie cutters, a meat thermometer, a battered game of Chutes and Ladders, a box boasting a tool that peels, cores, and slices apples.

RULES TO LIVE / 51

"What are people thinking?" Lindy asks, prepared to provide her own answer. "This is the most useless assortment of crap I've ever seen. Check this out." She holds up a tiny hourglass and places it on the table next to Mary so the sand begins to run down into the bottom funnel.

"Enough already," Mary says, knocking the hourglass over with one of her feet.

"Candles and a corkscrew. *Perfect*," Lindy says, pointing to the sign above the washer and dryer: NO OPEN FLAME OF ANY KIND. NO ALCOHOL.

"Yeah, whatever. It's your nails no matter what," Mary says. She holds up a foot for our inspection. Mary believes that whatever happens, look good at all costs. The only time she cried was when she discovered she'd left her favorite lipstick—Rusty Rose—at home. "You can't get it just anywhere," she said, then quickly dabbed at her eyes with a Kleenex to catch the running mascara.

I sympathize with Mary's obsession with what's right in front of her, what she can see, what she can touch. Here in my third week, I speak carefully, over and around the details of my recent life with Jonathan, which seem beyond truth, beyond words. They are no longer just part of a story I tell, the story of how at the start I mistook jealousy for love. Instead, "Your nails look fabulous," or "You look a little thin, bony around the hips." We all talk primarily about the way we look, how we fill our skin. We line up to stare at our faces in the bathroom mirror, apply a tube of half-used lipstick rescued from the bottom of the cardboard box marked Shelter Makeup. We parade around for each other like stood-up teenagers desperate for someone to notice the predicament we're in, the makeup a silly, useless weapon here where there are no men. Social anxiety exists here like anywhere else where people live communally, lurking under the surface of every exchange. We wander through the rooms of the shelter checking on everyone else, making sure no one has found a better form of distraction, making sure everyone is as miserable as we are.

The first night I was here, a woman called after me, "Hey, Maria, wait up," and for a minute I felt wrapped in the strange comfort of a familiarity meant for someone else. "Oh, sorry," the woman said when I turned around, not Maria. I had reached the point where I was willing to settle for recycled tenderness.

Lindy holds up her watch to indicate five minutes until ten o'clock. "I hope there's an intake," she says, laughing a little to show she feels guilty for saying it. She counts on the holidays, the season of peak family violence, to keep the counselor otherwise occupied so that the rule that says in our rooms by ten won't be a priority.

"Nice," Mary says, "real nice." She flicks a toenail paring toward Lindy.

Lindy pulls up the legs of her jeans like a man in a suit about to sit down and squats by the bottom of the tree. She puts her finger in the top of the pole where the top of the tree is supposed to fit. Lindy hates to see things unfinished. The half-built birdhouse she left at home agonizes her. She carries the instructions in her pocket, a black pen mark underneath the step where she left off.

The rain has stopped as suddenly as it began. Through the window I watch as Anna wades slowly in her slippers through ankle-deep mud toward one of the courtyard picnic benches. Her two children, a seven-year-old boy and a four-year-old girl, circle her, splashing. Their toy guns shoot suction-cup darts that are supposed to stick but instead fall flat on the wet cement sidewalk. Joan's dented-head little girl runs out to join them, making a gun out of her own hands, but Joan calls her back. Once she reaches the bench, Anna riffles through her bathrobe pocket for her cigarettes. A counselor rushes over, offering her a light, straddling the other side of the picnic bench, nervously centering the coffee can ashtray on the tabletop between them.

"I hope my husband gets shot so I can walk around in my bathrobe and counselors run after me to light my cigarettes," Mary says, looking out the window. This afternoon Anna got a call from her mother in the Mexican town just over the border that Anna and her children had fled. Her mother told Anna that her husband had been shot and killed by another drug dealer. A counselor was brought in to tell the children just home from school while Anna hyperventilated in a back room. We all watched as the little girl, her arms still through the handles of her backpack, followed the counselor into the crisis room. When the counselor told the children their father was dead, the boy laughed and laughed. We could hear him though the door was closed. He couldn't stop laughing.

His laughter was like a sealant he sprayed all around the room, covering himself. Nothing more would ever get in.

While Anna smokes, the boy pretends to fall down dead in a puddle. Anna doesn't seem to notice. She continues to smoke as another woman comes out of her room to scold him. "It was his stepfather, right?" Mary asks Lindy because Lindy knows everything about everyone.

"No," Lindy says, correcting her severely. "Anna was married to one man her entire life, since she was seventeen." Lindy still respects the sanctity of marriage.

Jonathan wasn't my first. I met him in my thirties, when I thought I finally knew what I wanted, when I thought I could offer the most. I was raised to believe that life adds up to something, that one experience meaningfully leads to another and eventually, someday, an epiphany. The irony is that on our first date, we talked about taking a trip to the desert together. We talked about camping out under the stars with coyotes howling in the safe distance, giant Gila monsters asleep on rocks cooled by the night. There was no question but that we were meant for each other, so to talk about taking a trip on our first date seemed natural. Remembering that feeling alarms me above and beyond everything else— that I felt so sure and so right when I was so utterly wrong.

That first night, I invited Jonathan in. While I put water on to boil for tea, he made me laugh by reciting rules for desert living he had learned on an Outward Bound trip. *Always inform someone of the planned destination, route, and expected time of return.* He spoke in a deep, put-on macho voice. *"Be sure the vehicle is in good condition and equipped with a sound battery, good hoses, spare tire and fan belts, necessary tools."* "Talk like yourself," I said, laughing. "Be Jonathan again and let's have some tea." But he didn't stop. *"If the vehicle breaks down, signal trouble by raising the hood, tying a cloth on the antenna."* I patted the space on the sofa next to me for him to join me. He leaned over to kiss me. *"Breathe through your nose,"* he whispered, still speaking in that other voice, *"don't talk, or lick salt if water is scarce."* I shivered with the best kind of pleasure—excitement laced with fear. When I woke up in the morning he was leaning on one elbow watching me. "You are the most beautiful thing I've ever seen," he said, speaking in his normal, Jonathan voice. "I don't know what I'd do without you."

Mary swings her legs, puts her feet on the floor, and starts on her fingernails with the knife. Still on her knees, Lindy sips from the flask she keeps in the inside pocket of her denim jacket, then squeezes toothpaste onto her tongue in case a counselor happens to walk in. She busies herself fitting the top pole of the tree into the bottom pole, then wraps the filler branches like long green pipe cleaners around the sparse areas of the plastic trunk. We've spent many nights like this, the three of us intent on something useless, waiting for a counselor to tell us to go to bed while other residents try to sleep. We strain not to listen beyond the rattle and hum of the swamp coolers.

I pick up the phone and dial the number to the airport. Lindy smiles at me—she knows about my phone calls.

Apparently it's been a long day for the man who answers the phone because he just says "What?" Still, the sound of his voice coming in over the line from the real world into the shelter lounge gives me a charge. Like the thrill I got—before Jonathan's on-the-half-hour phone calls; before he started checking the mileage on the car on the days he left it at home and walked to work and then stopped leaving the car at home altogether; before I started sleeping in my clothes because a nightgown somehow meant I'd been waiting for someone else; before Jonathan became so afraid each time I left the room that he'd flip chairs jumping out of them to follow me; before the beginning when those flipping chairs were the fast, loud proof of his love; before I'd ever met Jonathan, when I would go out to the airport though I wasn't flying anywhere. I watched the planes boldly defy gravity. From a bench, I studied people gliding on the moving sidewalks on their way somewhere, moving easily between one world and another.

The man's voice on the phone—coming from out there where he checks luggage or tears tickets to faraway destinations—makes my features sharper. I can feel the way my nose sits on my face and the hairs on my cheek brush against each other. I can hear my life happening, the scrape of Mary's knife and the clinking of glass Christmas balls in Lindy's hand. The table under my hand is just that, solid wood, nothing to interpret. The man hangs up. There is no bridging the gap between out there and our unlisted number, our P.O. box address.

Lindy saves the homemade decorations for last, putting

them to the side in a pile. She holds a Christmas ball up to the tree, deciding how to arrange them. She hangs another ball on a plastic branch, then pulls herself up from her knees and stands back to take a look. It is only at times like this, when she brushes her hair back from her face, that the yellowing bruise on her forehead is apparent. She walked into a wall trying to get out of her house quickly, before her husband came home from the police station. Once, she bent over in the kitchen to retrieve a dropped napkin and I saw the beginning of the zipperlike knife scars on her back from nights she didn't make it out in time. When I squinted my eyes, the scars looked like a ritual scarification, deliberate patterns meant to be deciphered. I touched her back without thinking, and she whipped around. "No," she said through her teeth. "I'm so sorry," I said, my eyes welling with tears for the first time since I'd arrived, afraid I'd lose my only friend.

She didn't talk to me again until the next morning. I asked her if I could tell her a story, and I told her about a day when my parents were still alive, when I was a child with my hand deep in the fur of our dog's coat, sitting on a dock as my parents prepared a boat. My parents laughed at my mother's soaked tennis shoes, at the ridiculousness of her stepping in the water accidentally, at the joyful ridiculousness of life in general. I buried my fingers in the dog's fur, smelled the sea air, and looked out at the ocean, endless like my life before me. "That's not a story," she said, but she wasn't judging me, just stating a fact.

I've seen my own bruise chart. It's blank—a line drawn through the front and then the back of an outline of a naked woman—except for an arrow pointing to the outline woman's wrists. "Self-inflicted" is written in parentheses. The woman's face is an empty circle without features. The slash marks on my wrist were a tentative rehearsal with a razor pressed into my flesh not hard enough to kill.

The night Jonathan discovered them, he was handsome and staid as a washed-up movie star. It was a month before I left, and I found comfort in the fact that someone this cruel could love me. His pupils pulsed larger and smaller until I felt hypnotized. He held my wrists, and for a moment it felt like a question. "This is no ordinary sorrow," I answered. His washed-up movie star looks encouraged the actress in me. He fingered the drawer of our bedside table that contained the gun bought for our protection. He was always stilling me with the possibilities, with my own wildest imaginings.

A Christmas bulb hanging from the end of one of the green plastic branches falls suddenly and shatters on the part of the lounge floor that the rug doesn't quite reach. Lindy pulls her pants up again and kneels to gather the shards of green glass. "I'm destined to spend my life on my knees," she says to no one in particular.

Mary admires the nails on her finished hand, and I dial my old number with the phone on the hook. Neither of us notices Lindy until she is standing in front of us. She holds her hand out like a child offering something she does not want anymore. A long sliver of green glass juts from the side of her wrist.

For the first time since I've known her, Lindy looks at me as if she doesn't know what to say. An accident like this is like nothing she ever expected or prepared for. "Please," she says quietly, looking everywhere but where the glass sticks out of the skin between the fleshier side of her wrist and the dangerous web of veins. "Please get it out." Her voice is small and polite in the face of this small violence.

Lindy has never asked anything from me, and even though what she's asking is obvious, I'm confused. But I don't turn my head the way Mary does; I stand up and take Lindy's hand.

"Get it out," Mary says as she slides down the couch, away from us. She puts the knife on the floor beside her. "Hurry up and get it out." She covers her ears as if we are all screaming. Then she is out the door and headed for the office.

I slide the glass out of Lindy's soft flesh slowly. The glass is barely lodged in her skin, but her fingers curve inward as I pull. The blood follows the glass to the surface and rushes out fiercely, though the cut isn't very deep. I remember Jonathan asleep after he'd exhausted himself. His breathing was the sound of waves ready to crash over me while I rested in cloudy bliss, my head rising and falling with his chest. I was always amazed to see Jonathan asleep, all that power shut down. The red of Lindy's blood is electric against the rest of this gray life. I stand and sit her down in the chair by the phone. She has her good hand to her face as if she's been slapped.

I grab up all the paper towels strewn around the

unwrapped Christmas ornaments, press them to Lindy's wrist, and as she opens her curled fingers we both watch the blood bloom across the white. The swamp cooler makes a noise as if something is trapped deep inside it. "Quiet," I say to the noise. "Quiet." My voice sounds as if I know what I'm talking about. I stroke Lindy's hair, and she closes her eyes. "Quiet." She seems grateful for the suggestion.

Burn smoky fires in the daytime and bright ones at night. One of Jonathan's Outward Bound phrases runs through my head. It's the same one that went through my head the day I left. I considered burning the house down, lit a match, then blew it out because I knew even then that I might want to come back.

When I push Lindy's hair back from her face, my fingertips brush the sprawling yellow bruise and I trace its outline. She pushes her head into my hand, resting it there. A new bunch of paper towels pressed to Lindy's wrist, we watch again as the red seeps thick through the white. The blood moves with a purpose, as if it were seeking me out for comfort.

I can already hear down the street the fire engine and the ambulance that come when the counselors call 911. The overnighter is new, and she must have panicked when Mary ran into the office. She walks in, followed by Mary biting her just-trimmed nails. Behind her are Joan and her dented-head daughter, Anna and her two children. The rest of the women are on their way. We all sleep without really sleeping, poised.

"Lindy, come up to the office," the counselor says sternly. She is young and pretty, and her tone of voice betrays her fear of the blood, of Lindy, of seeing so much of our lives she won't recover from it. Lindy opens her eyes slowly and looks at me as if she is about to tell me a crucial piece of information.

"I can tell she really cares," Lindy says instead, fake and sweet as the put-together Christmas tree. She shrugs toward the counselor, who is fiddling with the knobs on the lounge washer, shutting the door to the dryer competently.

"Press hard." I give her a new bunch of paper towels as the counselor comes over to help her up. Mary stands nearby, shifting from one foot to the other.

Urgent exhaust rises from the ambulance and the fire engine outside the gate. I imagine someone calling into the shelter from out there to listen to my own urgency—a woman from her burrow in the snow to tell me in her icy language that it is better to dig deep into the frost than to stand around and wait for someone to let you back in. When I go back to my room, I wrap the razor I stole from the office in a wad of toilet paper and flush it down the toilet.

Later that night Lindy knocks on my door. Her wrist is bandaged, as if she's been rescued. Everyone has retreated to her room except Mary, who slipped out the gate with the paramedics to meet her boyfriend at the biker bar. Lindy and I walk out into the courtyard and lie down in the damp sandbox under the glow of the shelter lights, swishing our legs and arms back and forth, making our own version of snow angels until our borrowed clothes are dark with wetness.

"The sky is like nothing I've ever seen before," Lindy says, still lying in the sand. Even though it's the same black sky that I saw through the window as I lay on Jonathan's chest hoping his deep, easy breathing would last forever or that it would stop quietly in the night, I know what she means.

On our third date, Jonathan drove me over the state border to prove that we could go anywhere together. The second time we made love, he bit my shoulder and broke the skin. Jonathan said the blood was love when love is everything, and when he said this I thought of how, when we'd driven over the state line, it had seemed for a minute insignificant. Once we'd passed over the line I'd thought—and then put it out of my head in the interest of romance—that the landscape looked just the same. More trees, fields, and small, slanted houses.

For now, I'm content to watch Lindy next to me holding her bandaged hand above her to keep it from getting wet, a flag of sorts to stake out our territory. We are any age looking up at the sky from the places we've made in the sand with our bodies digging deeper.

Honey, darling, sweet pooch," my mother calls from down-stairs. "Sweet darling, honey, pooch." Her voice does not waver as she bends down to pick some discarded thing up off the floor, spot-cleaning the house though she's meeting her date at a restaurant. "Honey, sweetie, darling." She's forgot-ten why she's saying these words, forgotten that she wants my attention. She is thinking of the evening ahead of her, whether to wear her hair up or down.

"What?" I call down from my old bedroom strewn with objects I used to love.

"I'm going out," she says, as if to say this is how you do it. I can hear her looking at herself in the mirror in the front hall, smoothing an eyebrow with an energy she hasn't had in years. She goes out almost every night after she gets home from her job as the administrator of the obstetrics division in a hospital. She meets men through the classifieds. I've learned these things since I came back home during a lull in my life, here at the age of thirty-one.

"You can recoup," she said when she invited me home upon hearing the news of my life, as if living without love or money were an illness. "Honey, sweetie, darling, pooch," she said, her words like outstretched arms.

I protested, though I knew what I had to do.

Now I come downstairs in the sweatsuit that I put on and stay in after I get home from work as a temporary in a graphics-design firm downtown. "Where are you meeting him?" I ask.

"Well-lighted, busy, don't worry," she says, putting on very red lipstick. Her powder clings to the soft hair on her cheeks. She has gotten her second wind of beauty ten years after my father died.

I step out onto the front porch with her, into the night and a neighborhood filled with houses exactly like this one, only backward on the inside. Across the street, Raymond stands in his kitchen window, pausing as he does the dishes to watch us standing on our porch.

"I'll call if it's late," my mother says, heading for her car. Her slips shows a little, but these days it's charming.

I wish sometimes that I were the one saying those words, that she were the one a little desperate for my attention. These days I am an actor trying to play a real person; I get all the lines confused.

In the living room, I settle in for the night with a glass of wine and near-stale potato chips I find forgotten in the back of the kitchen pantry by the briquettes. This is how it's been for weeks now. I don't need the *TV Guide* anymore to tell me what's on each night. Most nights I lose myself in the endless loop of half-hour shows. Lately I'm trying to limit myself to the shows I really like, the ones I think I can learn something from: a girl who comes to realize that her brother is envious rather than just plain mean, a father who learns that his goals for his daughter may be different from his daughter's goals. My goal is to watch only the ones that I can apply to my life, though I haven't figured out yet which ones those are.

On the coffee table there's an old photo album that my mother brought down from where it was folded into towels in the linen closet by the bathroom. She brought it down so that I could look at pictures of myself as a baby, pictures of me learning to walk, climbing up on the toilet, mouthing baby food from a spoon. I suspect that she wanted to show me these pictures because they are evidence that I have accomplished something and that, quite possibly, I will accomplish something again. What interests me, however, are the pictures of my mother. She is slimmer and wears sleeveless dresses that end above her knees. In one picture, five years younger than I am now, she looks coyly out from behind her wedding veil while her mother stands in the background feigning irritation. The picture that I always return to is the picture of my mother at age thirty-three in a dashing, jaunty hat. She sits on a park bench with pigeons at her feet. Her head is turned, and the profile of the long slope of her nose, like a gentle root erupting, is the center of the picture. She looks so sure of herself that it makes me wonder how she got that way.

When I lived at home before, my mother wore a clouded face full of apology—sorry dinner is late, sorry your father is dying, sorry for always being sorry. Now she is dashing once again like the picture, dropping her keys on the way to the car, wiggling her hips playfully as she bends to pick them up. In that picture, I am an idea that she will have a year later.

I hear a rustling on the front porch, the sound of scratchy polyester pant leg against scratchy polyester pant leg, and there is Raymond from across the street—timid, as if he weren't a regular guest when my mother is not here. Raymond is a little bit in love with my mother. When Raymond first moved into the house across the street, she invited him to dinner. He left a small bite of each thing—carrots, mashed potatoes, chicken—on his plate at the end of the meal, an offering, and he didn't say a word. Now when Raymond and my mother see each other from across the street or pass on the sidewalk, Raymond looks down, nods his head quickly in restrained acknowledgment of what my mother will never offer him. He likes to come over and occupy the space where my mother was or will be soon again.

"What's on TV tonight?" Raymond asks. He's told me that he doesn't have a television, but twice when I was locked out and went over to use the phone I saw the inside of his house, the exact opposite of ours, with the stairway to the left instead of to the right. Raymond's house does not have very much furniture, but it does have a sofa and a television that remained on and unwatched both times I used the phone.

"Come in," I say. I am not threatened by Raymond because of his crush on my mother. He was not around when I was growing up in the neighborhood, and we don't know much about him except what we see as the people who live across the street: he looks slightly older than my mother because he tries to hide his gray hair with a thick black formula; he washes the same set of dishes every night (this detail we guess), holding them up to the light in his window to make sure they are clean; and he checks his mail three times a day although the postman comes only once, at three in the afternoon. My mother often wonders aloud whether he is waiting for a winning sweepstakes or a letter from someone who has never written him before, because he never seems to get any mail or send any letters himself. Some days when we see him heading down his grassy slope to the mailbox with the American flag painted on it, my mother will say in a dramatic, drumroll sort of voice, "Could it be the winning sweepstakes?" She has that kind of energy.

Even though I am not threatened by Raymond, I turn on the light in the living room where the TV has been casting patterns of light on the wall. After he fixes himself a scotch and soda, Raymond takes a seat on one end of the couch and I take my old place near the other end. When Raymond comes over, I choose what we watch randomly and for the first half hour we do not speak, not even during the commercials. Flickering images fill our eyes until, after the first family plot in which a wayward daughter does right, Raymond speaks about my mother.

"I was thinking about telling your mother about the boy who comes to do my yard," he says tonight. "I was thinking that she might want him to do your yard too. The boy has a nice touch." From the table he picks up the picture of my mother looking out from behind her bridal veil. "That's a pretty picture," he says, crunching ice, and then we watch family plot after family plot until the ten o'clock news.

"How's your grandmother?" Raymond asks, a little of his drink spilling over the side of the glass as he raises it to his lips. Raymond doesn't know my grandmother, but he asks the question as if he is a friend of the family. It seems out of the blue, but he's looking at a picture of me, my mother, and my grandmother, standing in that order in front of a ride at the local fair. The ride is called the Twister, comprising two baskets that twirl like eggbeaters. A girl in my junior high class threw up while the ride was going full speed. In the picture, the three of us are pretending to be dragged toward the stairs to the Twister as if by some invisible force. My grandmother has placed her panama hat on the ground several feet away, as if the invisible force has blown it off and it landed there. My mother and I have our hands above our heads, eyes bugged. Behind us all, the Twister is a mere yellow blur, people strapped to the sides of the baskets, trying to resist its pull and twist.

"She's been dead for years," I say, remembering the way my mother was sorry about that too. My grandmother was unhappy with my mother in the end for losing her husband to an illness. She was upset that there was a pause in my mother's life after my father died, as though by taking too deep a breath, my mother might have passed out.

"Hmm," Raymond grunts thoughtfully, not particularly regretting the question. When the news is over, Raymond rises to leave. He takes his glass into the kitchen and then stands in the living room for a minute, looking at the picture of me, my mother, and my grandmother.

"The Twister?" he asks, pointing at the yellow blur though he is looking at my mother. "You all look alike," he says, running his finger along the row of us.

I slide down the couch to look, and it's true, we do. We are variations on a theme: the same thin hair and saucer eyes, the same exaggerated poses and looks of mock astonishment. I'm not sure why I'm so suprised. I've looked at these pictures over and over again since I've been home, but Raymond's looking at them has made me look again—the way he searches my mother's image for the source of her magic.

"That boy who does my lawn, he's really good," Raymond says. He is out the door and into a night filled with the hum of telephone wires and occasionally the sound of a faraway car carrying someone home. He walks across the street and into his backward house, and I imagine the sound of his shoes landing on the linoleum as he kicks them off, sits down on his couch, and flicks on *his* TV.

I take a glass of wine upstairs with me and drink it in bed with the lights off while in my head I pick out an appropriate outfit for work the next day. Sometime later I hear a car, then a key in the door, and then my mother's whispering voice and that of a man's. I hear my mother in the kitchen, probably putting the kettle on the stove to boil while maybe she sizes up this man, measuring her desire for him. Since I've been home is the first time that I've really, truly imagined my mother having sexual desires, and each time I imagine it I receive a small shock, as if some foreign source is administering charges to let me know this is forbidden territory. I listen to the hushed tones of my mother and this man as I finish the wine and set the glass by my bed next to the other glasses from other nights. It is the moments when the low tones turn to carefully suppressed laughter—at a minute gesture of my mother's or a joke told by the man that I cannot hear, something silly and quickly forgotten but shared between them— that I am most an outsider in this house. I lie in such a way as to be the smallest that I can be, heading for sleep while downstairs my mother's life continues.

The graphics-design firm where I work is sponsoring a benefit ball for cancer research. This is what my father died of, so I try to use this to help me feel more involved. My job as their temp is to handwrite the names of the guests on one thousand invitations. They learned from the agency that I know a little calligraphy, and they think it would be charm-

ing for a graphics-design firm to have handwritten invita-
tions. That sometimes the pen gets away from me is all right
with them—it's that much more of a personal touch. For the
past week now I've been sitting at a desk in the middle of the
office, balancing each invitation carefully on a clutter of
papers and slowly, carefully carving out a name. The other
women in the office call me by the names of past temps and
generally don't notice me as they discuss seating arrange-
ments for the dinner preceding the ball.

"Boy, girl, boy, girl doesn't work when there's less boys
than girls," the tall blond with the baby-doll bangs says
today. It's been the main argument all week.

"Wouldn't you know, less boys than girls?" the short red-
head says. She doesn't have pictures of a family taped above
her desk, though she does have several of a dachshund.

"I just do not want to sit next to you-know-who," says the
blond, mouthing you-know-who rather than saying it out
loud. I admire her drive, the way she knows where she
doesn't want to sit.

As they discuss whether sequins are too much, I have the
dangerous feeling that I often get at work. The feeling is
similar to dreaming that I'm going to do something against
my will, such as stay in my mother's house forever. It's like
the invisible force dragging us toward the Twister in the
picture, which I've always thought of as somehow real; the
fact of the picture itself has brought a reality to the pose,
when the pose was just something my father shouted from
behind the camera.

The blond scratches the back of her head with nails stiff and effective while she determines where she will sit. Deep down, she is acting too. I'm beginning to suspect that, deep down, all desire is faked. I imagine tearing the picture of me, my mother, and my grandmother into tiny pieces and throwing them out the window with the invitations to flutter and land randomly. Pieces of our faces pushing through the air while the sky falls away. There would be no telling where it would all end up, but it would be anything but predictable. It would be something to counter this endless process of recovery—my grandmother wanting my mother to recover from my father's death and now me, recovering from a badly scripted life. As my mother moves toward the vacancy left by my grandmother, and I move through my mother's cast-off ages, I wonder how one recovers from making a life.

The blond leaves the room for a minute and then comes back to say that the Xerox machine isn't working again. I look up because I know this has something to do with me. Within minutes I am out the door with an armful of speeches for the benefit ball that begin "Welcome ladies and gents" and "What a wonderful crowd we have gathered here tonight."

Despite the new braided tail down his back, I recognize the guy behind the counter at the copy place. He's someone I went to high school with, maybe I had a crush on him. His facial features have grown with his body; they are grotesque. I make my copies quickly in a corner and hope to leave the store unnoticed, but he comes from behind.

"I know you," he says, "I know you," like he's blowing my

cover. He leans against the copy machine and tells me how his band broke up a few years after college, how his girlfriend had a baby and left him a year later for his old drummer, how they all run into each other around town and it's a bad scene. Man, he says, and even though I hardly knew him in high school, he is looking to me for comfort. I copy my hand by accident.

"Better watch that," he says as a black-and-white version of my palm slides out of the machine. "Stuff's radioactive." I could take him home, and maybe we'd push against each other hard for a few hours, straining to find meaning in skin. We'd be new to each other but still safely anchored in the familiarity of high school. I start to count on my fingers how many years till I'm thirty-three. It's a goal I've set for myself, to start to take responsibility for my life then—I'm only two fingers away.

I pay for the copies quickly and head out of the store.

"See you around," he says in a way that makes me suspect he is watching me walk.

When I get back to the office, I carve my initials into the leg of my desk with a pen. I am a crazy teenage rebel trying to leave a physical mark in this office, and on this earth.

I call the community health center from work at my second fifteen-minute break. After the third loop of the same menu— self-esteem, assertiveness training, eating disorders, healthy relationships, body image, healing workshops—I get a real person on the other end of the line.

"Can you describe this pain in more specific terms?" the voice asks. It is a high, female voice that sounds as if it is coming through a wind tunnel, like this is someone who has used nose spray wildly. Her nostrils are hairless and smooth.

I begin to try. I explain that it feels something like when the gynecologist checks my ovaries, one hand inside and one pressing from the outside, as if but for my skin, the doctor would have an ovary in her hand. I tell her it's like that but not quite. I tell her that the pain seems to float in the abdominal area, that I'm worried it may land and become something serious, in which case what will I do?—I'm only a temp and have no health insurance. I tell her that sometimes I have delicious fantasies in which this pain does in fact turn out to be something tragic and this fatal diagnosis slices the fatty part off of my days until they are sculpted and meaningful. I begin to tell her that the pain began sometime in this last year, two years before I turn thirty-three like my mother in the picture, when my father was still alive and I was not even born, but the woman is giving me another number. It is the number of a counselor who she thinks would be better able to help me. I say this pain is my own personal damage, but the woman continues to give me the number. I pretend to take it down, saying it back to her at the speed that I would be writing it if I were actually writing it. My fifteen-minute break is over. Someday soon I will go down to the community health center and have a physical, though I worry that I might be disappointed to discover that this pain doesn't set me apart at all.

• • •

My mother is doing a hot-oil treatment for her hands when I get home from work. She has another date with the man from the other night.

"He was a real gentleman," she says, one hand in a hot pot of oil. She's had some losers from the classifieds—young guys who wanted Mrs. Robinson types, a guy who split his pants on the dance floor—so this is a high compliment. With a wooden spoon she ladles the oil over every inch of her hand up to the wrist. As soon as she takes her hand out of the hot pot, the oil becomes a pink wax glove. She takes one of my hands and dips it. It's burning hot at first, but then my hand starts to tingle as if it were electric.

"He speaks Italian," she says and dips my other hand. "He ordered in Italian at dinner." She says this shyly and cocks her head in a way that has evolved from a day years before I was born. Maybe she was walking down the street and did it accidentally—or on purpose, when a family like the one she didn't have yet walked by or she was thinking about a lover. She caught her reflection in a store window, briefly, and saw herself years from then.

"A romantic," I say, smiling, and I help her dip her other hand. We sit quietly at the kitchen table looking at our pink wax gloves, until there is a knock at the door.

My mother stands up and then holds up her hands, says, "How will I open it?"

It's Raymond, who didn't see my mother's car parked on the street instead of in the driveway. "I'll come back later," he says through the window. "I didn't mean to disturb you," he says, looking only at my mother's hands.

"The door's unlocked," my mother says. "Just push." She's laughing and having a good time, and I'm beginning to think I have a crush on her too.

Raymond finally pushes the door open. I convince Raymond, who is sure that my mother is laughing at him, to have a seat at the kitchen table.

"Wax dip?" I ask, but he shakes his head.

"The last thing I need is soft hands," he says. We all smile instead of laughing out loud because it is suddenly so quiet with the three of us sitting around the hot pot on the kitchen table. Outside, the sky slowly darkens all around the neighborhood, all around town.

"I should go," Raymond says. "I forgot what I came for." My mother walks him to the door. She tells him to come by anytime, though he already has. Through the window I watch him cross the street, moving through time with all his clumsy yearning. Those moves are not so foreign. When my mother returns to the kitchen table, we slide the wax gloves off whole. Our hands are left greasy, and the wax husks sit empty on the table between us, each with its distinct imprint of vein, knuckles, age, and time. Years from now, when these days spent at home with my mother blend together and seem small, this night will distinguish itself from the rest.

DIRT

DELIA is dreaming that her husband, Austin, stands above her on the bed, contorting his features into a face that might at any moment stick out its tongue. He wiggles terrible fingers at her. This is not the first time, and tonight Delia wonders, in her dream, if it's a dream at all. The thought scares her because he is the only person she knows in this new place full of dust and impossible sunshine.

When Delia wakes up, Austin is standing at the foot of the bed, already sweating in the soaring early morning temperatures. He is just out of the shower, but what is simply water and what is perspiration is as indistinguishable to Delia as her days in this house filled with a dead woman's belongings. Delia spends her days drinking bottomless cups of tea as she carefully fingers objects: the giant ladle that hangs above the kitchen sink, the remaining sliver of English Lavender soap in the bathroom, the pictures of dead relatives, Austin's aunt now among them.

The house is a gift to Austin, willed to him fully furnished by his favorite dead aunt. Delia feels the imprint of the old woman's bones in the bed that she and Austin share. The bed is the wedding bed of some ancient betrothed couple, which makes Delia feel somehow improper as she sleeps. On the headboard, enclosed in an oval of faded blue, is a small painting of the bed's original owners, then young and newly married, joining hands in profile. The woman has one long red spit curl, which Delia traces every night in an attempt to find the courage to fit herself into someone else's surroundings the way Austin says he has.

"You need to get out," Austin says, roughing his fingers through his hair to dry it. A small lizard clings to the wall behind him. Delia thinks she can hear it trying not to breathe; she sees its small, ticking pulse in the loose skin of its neck. Throughout the first week, Austin tried to show Delia what was wonderful about the house. Just yesterday Austin pointed out a china teapot decorated with tiny blue flowers that could never actually grow in this desert. He picked the teapot up from its brown and white crocheted doily in order to show Delia the detailing. As he lifted the lid, tiny black spiders spilled over the side like some dark liquid. This is a place where people are longing to end up, Austin had told her, denying the spiders with the urgency of his voice. He said it as if coming to this place had been the plan all along, then replaced the lid, catching several black legs underneath. He had gestured toward the window where Delia could see their leathery-faced old neighbor as she watered the spiky plants outside her house from a plastic milk jug. The water seemed to pass from the mouth of the jug directly into the thirsty air.

"I'm leaving," Austin says, shifting his weight impatiently from one leg to the other as he fools with a shirt cuff. He had signed himself up with a temporary agency the minute they arrived, eager to be productive even for somebody else's benefit. His current assignment is floor at a department store's going-out-of-business sale. He sorts towels in the bath section, discerning Sea Foam from Mint. He tells Delia he is pleased that he fits in with his fellow workers, that his boss commented on his "drive," that in this way he is on the right track to permanent employment. Delia wonders at the way Austin has settled so quickly. She is astonished at the ease with which he holds up objects in the house to her, as if they had always been his and not left behind.

With her own tentative fingers, Delia feels the sponginess of her arm. She is bloated, like a cactus storing water. She looks at Austin's fingers playing with his shirt, and yesterday afternoon drifts back to her like a vision seen through heat lifting off a highway. Delia had been reading on the couch printed with giant red peacocks in the living room while Austin opened drawers in a nearby table. He'd found an old telephone message that his aunt had written down and said something about how interesting it was that these frivolous

things lingered after death. Delia was not paying much atten-
tion until she began to feel sure out of the corner of her eye
that Austin was making a face. It was a child's face that said
she did not belong, as if she were another child who was too
thin or too tall, too fat or too short, and always unable to play
the game other children demanded she play. Austin's head
seemed to rock back and forth like a just popped jack-in-the-
box, but Delia could not look up to see if this was true.

"I'll go for a walk," she says to Austin because she knows
he hates her fear, and because she is afraid. Austin's shirt
clings to his damp back as he goes down the stairs without
saying good-bye, and Delia knows their relationship has
changed. "I'm the sort of person who won't do anything
great," Austin used to say. "Excitement happens in other
places, not in my life. There's nothing that says it has to."
Delia remembers when Austin first said this to her years ago
across a table in a diner, an elbow resting dangerously near
spilled mustard. His younger face did not mean what he said.
Then, Austin anticipated greatness; he'd expected excite-
ment. His eyes revealed he knew he was saying something
clever but she knew by the steadiness of his voice that they
would be married, and something inside her relaxed so that
she was able to take in the detail of the waitress's creased
face when she came over to ask if they had everything they
needed.

When Austin got the news that his aunt had left him a
house in the desert, suddenly it was if they were being called
to the place where excitement was. He embraced Delia as if

trying to squeeze some secret meaning out of her. Delia saw the way Austin had become more and more afraid that he was, in fact, the sort of person who would not do anything great, that he'd become the very person he'd tried to ward off by saying it out loud. Delia saw that Austin equated the movement from the East to the West with accomplishment. The house was something to move toward, something to move into. Now Austin is impatient with the way she doesn't unpack her bags or send out change-of-address cards. He is frustrated by the way she will not look for a job and the way she reuses one cup, one plate, and one set of silverware like some timid guest. He is anxious for her to adjust, as if it is she who is keeping them from the greatness and excitement that is due Austin. So he brings her bright cactus fruit. Certain Indian tribes make jam from this stuff, he says, and she knows this is something he was told by the man in the nearby plant store where he goes to get his facts straight.

Delia is made uneasy by the hostile thorns of the plants that surround this home. She does not want to live with spiders and lizards that crawl into the teacups for cover. The sun shines constantly over all of it, blindingly cheerful. "You worry yourself needlessly. Don't think in such grand proportions," Austin says as he leaves to sort the cotton-combed towels from the extra fluffy. He explains to her that studies have shown that sunshine cures depression. Delia wonders about this on the days that she watches her leathery-faced neighbor sit in her gravel yard, sprawled in a beach chair so far from the ocean. Every day Delia watches her neighbor turn her face to a sun that can no longer penetrate her rough skin.

Delia hasn't always been afraid. As a child, she yearned for horrible things to consume her body and her life. She envied the little girl in her second grade class who went suddenly deaf and was kidnapped by her stepmother. When the little girl was returned to her rightful home, people looked at her with concern, unable to ask how she was except with futile hand gestures that meant nothing in the sign language that the girl was still struggling to learn. The little girl smiled in a way that showed she was braver than anybody. Delia would have liked the attention this girl received as someone who knew something of the world. Now Delia's body swells to protect itself from its environment. Her skin seems thicker. Now she spends hours at a time waiting for the sound of a surprise—a popped cork, a crumpling bag as someone unpacks a cake—to tell her their new life is just distraction leading up to the surprise, something to tell her this is a practical joke and not really her life.

Outside there is the chirring of a bug that Austin does not yet know the name of while inside Delia sways tremulous like a flame before reaching for the broom. In the mornings she sweeps up the tracked-in dirt. The dirt is everywhere. Here, everyone's yard is dirt. Delia has noticed that her leathery-faced neighbor sometimes arranges her dirt with a broom, brushing it back and forth, stirring it up into a small brown cyclone around her. The dirt sticks to Delia's damp, hot skin and she tastes grains of it between her teeth.

Delia turns on the radio as she sweeps, to a news program about two brothers who both play classical guitar. Delia listens through the swish of the broom to the announcer, who says that the brothers perform one piece together, one brother's arms wrapped around the other from behind as they both pick at the same guitar to play the same song. The brothers, according to the announcer, start and end the song at exactly the same time with no apparent signals. Delia pokes at a thick cobweb as the announcer says that even the brothers find it strange. She imagines this is what a good marriage should be and searches in her mind for a moment like this between her and Austin, but all she can come up with are the terra-cotta hands sticking out from the wall in the News and Gifts airport shop. Delia and Austin's flight from the East had stopped in Denver, and they had stepped into the shop to buy a newspaper. The terra-cotta hands reached out from the wall on shortened forearms, offering books from some anonymous source. This is what Delia is reminded of as she brushes at her face with her own quick hands for something that isn't there.

Delia steps out the door to go for a walk so that she can find something to bring back to Austin to say that she has left the house. As she shuts the door behind her, she has a vision of Austin, almost unrecognizable, prancing from one foot to the other on her side of the bed. He points at her with first one index finger and then the other, smiling wide like a clown in what seems like a dream and which Delia now recognizes as the dream that she had several nights ago. Next door she sees a curtain in a front window move and knows her neighbor has watched her venture out. The dirt in her yard is in a flurry from her sweeping; gold flecks sparkle in the sun that has wrapped itself around the day. Delia goes left instead of right when she reaches the end of her street because she has never gone that way before and because she worries that if she goes right, it will disturb her not to recognize what she's already seen. Jesus rises up all around her, black and brown and yellow, in the painted murals of her neighborhood.

Delia kicks a stone that someone has painted blue, past festively colored stucco houses guarded by dogs that give a few obligatory barks and then lie down again. She kicks the stone down the middle of a street with no cars and feels the sweat run down her back in salty streams. She feels certain that she once felt passionately about her life but pictures only a girl she glimpsed in a china store where she worked before she met Austin. The girl carefully touched a small china elephant under a sign that read PLEASE DO NOT HANDLE. She touched it with her long fingers like delicate tentacles, sensing something important about not only the object but the gesture itself.

The blue-painted stone disappears into the open doorway of a creaky one-story house like any other on this street. SNOWCONES, TOYS, ANTIQUES reads a sign over the door, and Delia remembers that she must bring something back to show Austin. She nearly trips over the hose that runs from a spigot on the front of the house around to a side pen where it shoots water into a bucket already overflowing. The water runs over the sides and floods the yard with puddles that turn dust to dirt. Chickens perch carefully on stones while two ducks sit in the puddles, trying to float. A brown and white goat trails his long beard through dirt and water alike.

A tall, thick man with hair parted at his ear, thin strands swept over his head, appears in the doorway. "Houdini," he says, nodding his head toward the goat, who now lowers himself into the mud. The man bends at his trunklike waist to pick up the painted-blue pebble. He slowly puts the stone into his mouth and rolls it back and forth between his cheeks before offering it to Delia. "This is not really blue," he says.

"Are you looking for something in particular?" a woman's voice asks before she appears to push the man out of the doorway with a familiar aggressiveness. He steps back laughing and pinches her arm with fingers that know just when to stop. She takes the blue stone from his hand and holds it up to the light. "This means you will travel." She takes it back to the counter where there are several rows of stones and a small book titled *Fortunes*.

"I've already traveled," Delia says, but still she looks into the front room, at the novena whose candleholders are filled with precariously balanced, dusty red goblets. Nearby is a dresser with drawers pulled out and filled with candy wrappers, pencils, and silverware. The floors of this room slant into another room stuffed with a vanity scattered with cigar boxes and atomizers made of different-colored tinted glass. Empty frames cover the wall over a TV that sits on wooden crates, turned on with no volume, as if someone almost lives here or has just left the room. On the screen an older woman and a younger woman gesture furiously at each other as their mouths open and close without a sound. Tiny feather dusters hang unused, for sale.

"I'm just learning," the woman says, indicating the *Fortunes* book. "Look around, it's all for sale."

The stones sliding around on the glass counter cause Delia to taste the salt of sea glass from someplace far away, from before she knew Austin's face. It is the taste of a time before she was fearful, when she still envied the deaf and kidnapped little girl. She thinks of the second day in the dead aunt's house. She carried her suitcases up the stairs with Austin carrying his close behind her. She stopped to get a better grip, and as she did she looked under her arm and there was Austin wearing a secret, wicked smile. He ran his fingers quickly through his hair, but she could have sworn he'd been giving her the finger.

"Gotta get back to love," the man says, as if it were a place, and he walks into a back room where Delia sees a love seat partially stripped. Every other piece of furniture in the room is unfinished, like somebody's abandoned New Year's resolutions.

"Let me try," the woman says, as if to say, "Let me try again," as if she's known Delia for years. "I've got it all arranged, according to your height and some liberties I've taken." The stones make zigzags across the counter. Delia is sure that the woman has abandoned the *Fortunes* book.

"Don't tell me," the woman says. "You're married." She laughs as Delia looks at her wedding ring. The woman's hands are covered with rings. One in particular catches Delia's eye. It has two dark blue stones in a serpentine pattern that seems to climb up the woman's finger.

"That's a beautiful ring," Delia says, touching a stone so smooth it makes her sleepy with contentment.

"These are for sale too," the woman says, spreading her fingers like a mannequin's. Delia thinks of the news story of the brothers who play classical guitar together. In this woman cutting deals with the world, Delia has found a similar moment of perfection. The rings must have flown in through the front door and slipped themselves onto the woman's fingers. Someday they will fly off her fingers and out the back door. The relationship the woman has with the rings has more to do with the way she reached up to take them from the air as they flew in the door than with the rings themselves. Delia pictures Austin's aunt wandering through the antiques store, opening and closing old cookie tins that once belonged to someone else. She imagines bringing the old teapot covered with flowers and filled with spiders and placing it anonymously among other people's martini glasses and clay angels. In her mind she walks through Austin's aunt's house and gives it all away, everything that Austin has held up to her.

"You have children," the woman says, then laughs and studies Delia's face. "You don't have children?"

The woman reaches for Delia's hand and holds it with her

own. "Let's give your palm a look," she says, and Delia hears the tall man in the back room begin to strip a piece of wood he probably hasn't touched in years. Delia closes her eyes, and the long fingers of the girl in the china shop reaching for the elephant return to her as if the girl were there with her now.

"You are tired," the woman says, in a voice that is not part of divining Delia's fortune. The woman leads Delia to a couch stuffed with rag dolls. A small doll foot pokes out of a tear in the arm.

Delia hears a rustling like paper moving across the floor. "Scorpions," the woman says. Still, Delia leans her head back on the couch, comfortable in this place where anything might go at any moment. Delia breathes easily with this woman willing to divest herself of worldly objects after she's worn them for a while. "Don't worry," the woman says, though Delia has already closed her eyes. "Scorpions carry an ancient toxin. We've built up an immunity over the centuries."

The woman picks a broad-backed silver brush from the top of the crowded vanity and sits beside Delia on the couch. As the woman slowly brushes Delia's hair, Delia does not dream the dream about Austin's twisted face. She will not go back there. Her decision is as ancient as the scorpion toxin, one she made long before she ever met Austin. She dreams instead that she is handling scorpions, tracing their curved and rustling bodies with delicate fingers. She dreams that she holds up a scorpion to the woman in the antiques shop and asks, "What is this?" "I'm not sure, but it could be worth millions," the woman answers as the sweet and ancient poison sinks deep into Delia, seeking out a secret beneath the sum of her experiences. She will take the scorpion and let it loose in the swirling dirt outside her neighbor's house. Once Delia's hands are free, she will push the leathery-faced woman in her beach chair all the way to the ocean.

INDULGENCE

Today is not even a holiday and we are waiting in swivel chairs side by side in front of mirrors lit by amber bulbs in a room done all in pinks at Well Hello, Beautiful. It is usually her birthday that is the occasion for visiting, but these days my best friend, Clarissa, finds other occasions—Thanksgiving, Christmas, and Saint Patrick's Day this year. Last month she said something about the vernal equinox but then came down for a week and never mentioned it again once.

Like me, Clarissa—who informed me when she arrived that she has changed her name to Rissa, and I did give it a day's effort, but she's Clarissa to me—is dressed in a wraparound black robe tied in front. We are both naked underneath except for our underwear, according to the instructions in the dressing room: DISROBE FOR YOUR OWN PROTECTION.

Our heads sparkle with strips of tinfoil. This process, one of Clarissa's ideas, promises delicate highlights with minimum regrowth difficulty. "Whatever," Clarissa says. "It's a necessary indulgence."

Under the bright overhead lighting, Clarissa and I both look slightly green. There are pink plastic domes attached to the backs of our chairs, whose arms are swung so the domes are not covering our heads. They hover like empty sockets over the floor in this room that smells like canned peaches. Other customers in black robes like ours sit under dryers reading magazines and consulting with salon attendants dressed in pink. The salon is a world unto itself.

"Beauty is more than skin deep!" Clarissa reads to me from the picture taped to the mirror in front of her. It is a picture of a cat with a flower-print dress on, applying red lipstick with an obviously fake paw. Clarissa slides one hand under her robe to her left breast the way she's been doing all day. "Still smaller than a bread box," she says of the lump discovered recently by her gynecologist during a routine checkup. I start to offer the hope that she offered me when she arrived, the possibility of the lump being fibrotic, but Clarissa has a way of talking as if to herself when she doesn't want to hear things. "Because you're worth it," she reads from another cat picture. In this picture, a cat with a blush brush in one fake paw and grapes in the other stands over a cat reclining on a divan.

"Do you think this woman is ever coming back?" says Clarissa, referring to our beauty consultant, Camille.

Clarissa looks down the V neck of her robe. "I definitely wore bad underwear. I think Zach took all my good underwear and then hoped I would be in an accident." Zach is Clarissa's most recent ex-boyfriend, whom I never met before they broke up two weeks ago. Clarissa is one of the few people I know who actually dates, and dates regularly.

"What kind of accident?" I ask, willing to contend. As long as she's on vacation, Clarissa says she doesn't want to talk about her real life. I can play this game too. I put on my newscaster's voice and say, "At Well Hello, Beautiful this afternoon, due to a freak shortage of robes, a woman was required to have her hair done in nothing but her really bad underwear."

Clarissa pretends to stick two fingers in her eyes.

"We're getting our hair highlighted. Our underwear is not the point," I say, seeking a little decorum.

Clarissa visits from a city bigger than this one where we both grew up. She moved after we graduated from the state college here. She's adventurous, always going places she's never been before. Lately, though, she says she does not feel rooted, and when she says it she uses her hands, wiggling her fingers as if they are roots settling in. She says the free packets of vitamins she gets as a telemarketer for a vitamin company have lost their charm. She says she is immune to the vitamins and they are actually making her sick now. She blames them for her current health problem. She suspects the lump in her breast is really a vitamin capsule. "I'm taking care of myself to death," she says. She blames her love life on the vitamins too. Zach, her longest relationship, lasted a month, and on his way out he referred to Clarissa as "the perkiest woman he ever met." Afterward Clarissa said she needed to visit somebody else's life, so she came to see me.

"Do you think this woman forgot about us? Leaving this on too long has got to damage your hair." Clarissa taps the sparkling silver on her head with impatient fingers.

"It's only been twenty minutes. She said thirty to thirty-five." I make up numbers to calm us both.

"I feel like a baked potato," Clarissa says. She picks up a magazine filled with haircuts and flips to the middle. There is a picture of a woman in a red jumpsuit with her hair cut midear and swept dramatically across her face.

"Don't we all deserve friends and marriage and love and children and jobs that satisfy us and good haircuts and nice clothes?" says Clarissa. "I can understand how having a few of those things might disqualify you from the rest, but really, don't you think?"

"I don't like that jumpsuit at all," I say. This morning when we had this conversation about what Clarissa's life lacks, I was the one who ended up feeling bad, which scared me because Clarissa has comforted me all my life.

Clarissa and I are longtime friends. Clarissa claims, though we didn't meet each other until junior high, that she and I have the same first memory. For me, it is a memory of being two, on a Donald Duck swing with an orange duck bill for a seat in Oak Tree Park. For Clarissa, it is a memory of being three and a half (she's that much older), on a Donald Duck swing with an orange duck bill for a seat in Oak Tree Park, watching another little girl, who was me, swinging on the swing next to her. These things are important, and true or not, Clarissa makes things up with the best of intentions. Once, in high school, she told me she had a dream in which God was her ex-boyfriend. I honestly believed she was that powerful; there are times even now, all grown up, that I still believe it.

Clarissa says she has come to visit my life, but here in this beauty salon we are doing what we always do when we get together—lifting ourselves out of real life even as we stare at ourselves in the mirror.

"Okay, the jumpsuit's hideous. But doesn't everyone deserve their health? Sturdy sinuses?" Clarissa says.

"Yeah, yeah, yeah." I'm relieved because sturdy sinuses is Clarissa teasing me. I'm a medical secretary and during my spare time in the neurosurgery clinic, I read patient files—spina bifida and brain tumors, pictures of shaved heads with stitches like the leather stitching on a baseball. Once, I read the medical report of a doctor who had just finished removing a brain tumor successfully, but with the slip of a scalpel he put the patient's sinuses out of commission. The report stated that, in order for this operation to be successful, "sturdy sinuses are a must." When I told Clarissa about the slipup in the operation she said, "That's perverted." She has a gift for malapropisms.

The irony of Clarissa's lump is that, of the two of us, I thought it would be me who would fall victim to something like that. I often go home from my job and run my fingers slowly through my hair, checking. The first time I did it I gave myself a scare, not realizing until I asked a doctor at work that skulls are by nature lumpy. I'm still never sure. I check my whole body for lumps, sometimes mistaking bone for something more tragic. My breasts feel like tapioca, always. It's this constant searching without results, good or bad, that Clarissa used to say made her wish she'd find something.

One day at work, as I stared out the window, I saw the wind blow a woman's red hat from her head. A light flickered on and off where I imagine my heart must be and when this happened I thought I understood the weight of Clarissa's constant search. I sometimes walk up and down the hall in my apartment thinking about that midair red hat against the gray sky as I check for any slight shift in my equilibrium.

When Clarissa visits, we reward ourselves. We sneak banana splits in Clarissa's roomy purse into movies during the middle of the day. We leave the theater, hands sticky with chocolate sauce, blinking into the sun as our eyes adjust. We go to the zoo and put peanuts on the long tongue of the giraffe. We love to watch the way it blinks its huge brown eyes and rolls the peanuts slow and sexy, one by one into its mouth.

Clarissa always has a plan like movies in the afternoon or coloring our hair. In junior high, Clarissa could memorize the class schedules of her crushes easily so that she would just happen to be walking by a particular doorway when a certain class let out. She is also the sort of person who knew how to leave something strategically, a scarf perhaps, at a boy's house so she'd have an excuse to come back later. She's quick on her feet that way.

Clarissa turns to me suddenly and says, as if she'd never seen me before in her life, "Well, hello."

At first I think she's reading the neon script WELL HELLO, BEAUTIFUL sign over the basins behind us that are visible in the mirror. But then I recognize the game we've been playing since we first met. When we were younger, one of us was the boy and the other the girl and we'd meet for the first time, but lately we play it as two women who haven't seen each other in a long time.

"Well, hello to you too, Lucretia," I say, making up a name. "It's been forever. What have you been up to?" I laugh, in an attempt to keep things light.

"Well, Priscilla," Clarissa says, "I left this town for a city with a nightlife, a place where there's always something to do."

"So you like it? I, as you probably know, am fresh back from Napa Valley where I was doing Robert Mondavi a little favor and leading wine tours. It's the life. You know, cheese and wine, wine and cheese. And you?"

"I started my own health spa. At first, of course, I was selling vitamins over the phone, but I moved up quickly." Clarissa is straight-faced. She picks up a comb from the faux-marble countertop and plucks at the teeth with her nails.

"It sounds fabulous." I drag the *a* for effect. "Did you hear

I'm engaged to one of the Mondavi brothers? Proposed right there in the vineyard. He said I was the bouquet he'd been searching for all his life." I giggle like a little girl. "The health spa?" I prompt Clarissa when she doesn't smile.

"Very elegant," Clarissa says. "Marble columns at the entrance, cool blue throughout." She pauses, sighing. "Mud baths, steam baths, bath baths. And piles of fruit and specially concocted vitamin drinks served to the customers on silver platters."

"You've come a long way from your small-town beginnings. And you live in a beautiful house, I imagine."

"The most," she says theatrically, running one finger quickly down the comb so the teeth whistle as they bend. Clarissa watches the comb as she does this, concentrating. "And I've had a thousand lovers and never loved a single one of them," she says. "Yes, it's true, I've escaped my small-town beginnings. . . ."

I dread the look that comes over Clarissa's face now, that look of helpless surprise in the face of what she is about to say or do.

"This is true," Clarissa says, her voice part movie actress and part the drama of her own natural voice. She smiles wickedly. She watches herself in the mirror as she runs a finger along her hairline where the tinfoil begins. "And I keep myself company in my exquisitely furnished apartment with the knowledge of my own success. I don't need a lover. I don't need anyone, and I'll die alone, eating kiwi and luxuriating in my own mud bath."

"Clarissa," I say.

"I don't even need friends," Clarissa says, in Lucretia's voice because she's electing not to hear me. "And that's Lucretia to you."

"Whatever your name is, enough," I say, afraid of the lump lying in wait deep in her breast, afraid of the inoperable tumor of loneliness that lies even deeper inside. I am angry that Clarissa won't talk about these things and terrified that she might.

"Did you decide there's no hope for us?" Clarissa says as Camille, our beauty consultant, returns in the pink splendor of her outfit. With her is another pink-aproned woman. Emery boards and combs stick out of the pocket of her apron in a chaotic and upsetting way.

I look at Clarissa's reflection in the mirror and almost don't recognize her not looking back at me. Sometimes when I'm walking up and down the hall in my apartment, I wonder what interesting thing Clarissa must be doing at that moment because she would never wander the hall aimlessly.

"This is my assistant, Jasmine," Camille says. "She's learning the ropes. I was thinking, if you ladies don't mind, that Jasmine and I could wash you two out together. Otherwise I'll do you one at a time, which of course will take much longer."

"That's fine," I say, immediately yielding to Camille's subtle hint. Clarissa looks at me sideways, as if I were a stranger she happened to be watching, and gives me a look that says, When will you learn to put up a fight? She doesn't just mean now, here at Well Hello, Beautiful. She means the way I've stayed in our hometown, the way I've settled into a job I found by accident, the way I let my fingernails and toenails grow wild and unshaped and don't even think twice about it. No matter how often I tell her that I'm content, she won't believe me. I never wanted to leave—but it's always been hard to draw the line between where her ambitions begin and mine end. She looks at me as if to say, Get out of this town already or next thing you know you'll have married Bobby Taylor who was voted most popular in high school and now works sorting Terra Cotta from Egg Shell in his father's paint business. Clarissa's look scorns my fairy-tale suspicion of someday finding something wonderful right here at home. Clarissa's look says all of this to me and includes the injustice of her own life not being much better. I fear that we will both tumble into the hole of Clarissa's fear.

Camille will do Clarissa, and Jasmine, her assistant, will do me because that's the way these things work out with me and Clarissa. Jasmine's fingers smell like the canned peach smell of the salon as she rests her hands on my tinfoil head, long nails gently scraping my scalp.

The four of us walk over to the pink basins on the other side of the room, where Clarissa and I sit down in reclining chairs and tip our heads back so that Camille and Jasmine can begin to unwrap the tinfoil.

"Slowly," Camille cautions Jasmine. "You don't want to jolt the follicles."

Clarissa slides her foot along the linoleum floor to mine,

making sure I caught this. She has decided to be herself again.

Jasmine tests the water from the hose with her fingers before she begins to wash the excess color out. The water runs over my ears so that for a moment I can hear only my own heart, its steady, persistent beat.

When she is done she wraps a towel turbanlike around my head. Camille has Clarissa done up in the same way. We are led back to our swivel chairs in front of the mirror, and Camille and Jasmine begin combing and blow-drying and teasing our hair.

"You're much redder," I say to Clarissa, meaning her hair.

She looks at me, and I notice for the millionth time since I've known her how beautiful she is with her thick charcoal-stroke eyebrows and her big square jaw suggesting a person who would never be left with nothing to say.

Clarissa puts her hand on her throat and starts to cry.

Camille keeps combing and teasing Clarissa's hair, having decided that I will handle this. She's opted for the this-isn't-happening approach.

"Sweetie," I say, horrified by the big tear rolling down Clarissa's cheek unchecked. Jasmine takes my face in both her hands, pointing me out to myself in the mirror.

"Done," she says. My hair is streaked with shiny blond. Clarissa's hair is dazzling as she finally brushes the tear away with her hand.

"I feel like a converted person," Clarissa says, recovering quickly, as we stand up to go change back into our clothes.

I will pay with a credit card and Clarissa will pay me in cash later. While I step up to the cash register, she walks over to a large gilded mirror to look at her hair. Above the cash register is a small mirror and I can see Clarissa behind me. She doesn't know I'm looking at her and she looks at her reflection the way I imagine she does at home, alone in her apartment. I've looked that way too, studying myself and longing to be studied.

I think about what will happen after this necessary indulgence. We'll go back to my apartment—shop for dinner and wine, pop popcorn, and watch a late night movie on TV, do exactly what we want—until Clarissa returns to her real life elsewhere with risk embedded in her breast and I go back to the comforting rhythm of work and home, work and home. For right now, though, watching Clarissa watch herself in the mirror, I love her in the same way I would love a landscape that is still and unselfconscious. These moments in my life are subtle as the new gold streaks through my hair. These tiny jewels are what I live for.

THE winter will ruin my life," Flora says out loud, standing alone in her kitchen near the small hole that allows her to see through to her landlord's kitchen below. "Ruin me, ruin me, ruin me." This is one among many things she rehearses saying to her landlord. She mimes cutting her heart out and throwing it down the hole into her landlord's kitchen. She imagines it landing, still beating, in his sink full of dirty bowls and spoons.

Cold air rushes into her lungs, and Flora pushes the speed dial on her phone to call downstairs to Rock—just Rock, not for Rock Hudson, not for rock 'n' roll, just Rock, as in stone, as in mountain, he explained to her the first time she called him to complain about something. He is eighteen and lives alone—Flora sometimes catches glimpses of his spiky hair through the hole; on her days off, she listens to him pour his bowl of cereal for breakfast, and again for lunch, and again for dinner. Flora has decided, after careful consideration, that she loves him.

His mother used to live in the apartment above Flora until very recently. Flora never heard a sound. She suspected the mother did not move once she was in her apartment; she imagined her sitting in a wooden chair, immobile. There were no problems—no leaks, no crumbling grout—when the mother was here. One day Flora heard her yell down to Rock, "The more I do, the more I hate." Flora couldn't imagine what she did sitting in that chair. "Then leave," Rock said flatly, and she did. Flora has decided that Rock would understand this important question: How old were you when you realized life didn't necessarily get better? She feels sure he understands that there isn't necessarily an accumulation, a building of one thing upon another, until you reach the end as your best self. She thinks he understands that you may in fact reach the end as someone quite different from your best self. You may even arrive at the end so many rungs down from your best self that you can't even see what your best self looks like.

A year ago Flora and her friend Peter ate in the same cheap Indian restaurant every night, talking about the directions their lives might take. Then Peter's life, like the lives of other friends of Flora's over the years, actually took a direction. His screenplay about lovable losers like himself and Flora was picked up; he was introduced to a crowd of formerly-nerdy-now-excruciatingly-hip writers; and he met a woman who was just like Flora only not Flora. Peter invited Flora to parties and screenings, but Flora found that she lost her bearings in public, that she couldn't be funny the way she could in private. She and Peter went back a few times to their Indian restaurant but it wasn't the same. Their relationship had revolved around possibility, not achievement, and they weren't equipped for the change. While Peter had been waiting to someday leave the confines of the restaurant for the bigger world, Flora had been happy sitting there at the table across from Peter.

There is a pulse of sound downstairs as Rock turns on his TV, which he often does, sometimes in the middle of the day, halfway through a soap. *Don't leave me but you must because we are in love, because we are related, because, because, because, don't leave.* Now the saccharine-sweet soundtrack—Jim Croce or someone trying to sound like Jim Croce—of a Sunday afternoon movie about somebody dying of an incurable disease drifts up through the hole.

Flora goes to the phone. She has learned the power of using the telephone, the way she can cradle Rock's voice against her ear. There were days, after all, when the phone was the only way to reach him, especially right after his mother left him and he wouldn't even answer the door. Often, Flora will put her ear to the hole in the floor to hear him opening a cereal box, or rearranging his toolbox, or humming a tune that sounds like wind caught somewhere. Then there is Flora's letter-writing campaign. With increasing frequency she composes eloquent diatribes on clogged drains, sporadic hot water, poor water pressure, chipping paint, the way the kitchen window doesn't fit in its frame and clangs in brutal wind.

Strangely, her interest in Rock, her love for him, manifests itself in complaints. She's like a little girl who shows she likes a boy by hitting him. She can't stop herself. These days a thin film of poison coats Flora's words whenever she speaks to anyone. It wasn't always like this. There was a time when Flora was considered funny, a real crack-up, but over the past year her sense of humor has gradually been stripped of its graceful acrobatics, its fanciful costumes. There is a nugget of rage at the heart of it that Flora has struck upon and she can't help touching it again and again, like checking a canker sore with her tongue. But today, she thinks. She is unable to finish the thought. She's not sure exactly what she has in mind, but today she will make true contact with Rock. The winter chill that has crept into her body wells up inside her like a storm.

"Uh-huh." Rock answers the phone, mouth full.

"Rock," Flora says. She wraps her mouth carefully around the word, hopes that he'll hear more than just his name in the way she speaks it. "Rock, have you seen the hole in my kitchen floor?" What she means is: Have you noticed my beating heart in your sink?

"Get to the point, Flora. I've got new tenants—a young married couple," and Flora wonders if he's emphasizing this to spite her. "They're moving onto the third floor any minute now," Rock says wearily. Then, pausing as if to decide whether to offer her the next sentence, "I haven't been feeling so well."

"I'm not giving you breaking news here, Rock. This is the same hole that's been here for a week now," Flora says, ignoring his complaint and raising him one. She's practiced other words in bed in the dark—*What kind of cereal do you like the best? Are you lonely?*—but they are lost inside of her somewhere. She peers down into Rock's kitchen to a single white tile with blue trim. She is not so sure that she wants him to fix it, or what it is precisely that she does want him to fix. She imagines Rock laying his spiky head in her lap and falling asleep, snoring a little. She'd shake him awake to tell him tenderly to be quiet.

"Listen, Flora, I really have something wrong with my head. Terrible headaches," Rock says, also the sort of person who doesn't need another person to carry on a conversation. With Rock and Flora, there is always one extra person.

"If you look at your ceiling, you will see what I mean," Flora says, waiting for Rock, who now stands right below her, to look up through the hole, but he doesn't. He moves, and there's just that one blue-trimmed tile.

"Every day for the past week I have headaches," Rock says.

"Don't think I don't know about you," Flora says, hanging up the phone. It sounds good, like she has something on him.

She looks out the window at the terrible cold sky going dark. The gray shadows of winter fill her with a boredom that drills into her bones. The world lit like the apocalypse at dusk. Every day threatens in its cold murkiness to be the last. She said this to the deli guy on her corner, but he just looked at her blankly and then stared past her to the next customer. She was practicing to say it to Rock because she suspects that he would appreciate the images she uses to articulate loneliness. This winter, cold air sneaks in through her ears, nose, and mouth and sets her on edge, makes her shiver from October until April, and she is not an old woman. She is still of marrying age, her cousin Carol said, hopeful when she called today, her obligatory Sunday call. Carol lives in the city, though Flora hasn't seen her in years. A year ago Carol became a devotee of a self-help guru among whose directives was: Find someone less fortunate than you and be charitable. So Carol calls each week to see if something miraculous has happened to Flora, and if nothing miraculous has happened, then Carol offers herself as that miracle. "You look thirty-seven," she said today. "Not a day older than thirty-seven." Flora is thirty-nine.

"I'm thirty-six," Flora said. "Thanks a lot. And besides, how do you know? You haven't seen me in years. I may have aged beyond recognition."

But she was sorry when Carol made an excuse to get off the phone.

Leaves mixed with gusts of city dirt blow mercilessly down the street. It makes Flora want to blame someone—the deli man who doesn't understand her and whose fruit is rotten; scaredy-cat widowed Carol, who sends checks faithfully (the self-help guru encourages this along with the monthly donation to the guru's institution); Samson, her boss at the art gallery where she works part time taking calls from creditors; the man who is pulled by his leggy Great Dane puppy down her street every morning. He once asked her the time, still moving as his dog dove into a hedge after some quick movement.

Life was always skittering away from Flora like that, diving into hedges. Her career as an artist. Well, those drawing classes she took until the instructor asked her in front of the entire class to draw something that we all might recognize. That man she met in the gallery who eventually slipped his cold hand down her shirt as if he were fishing for forgotten change in a pocket. Without meaning to, when he asked for the time, she scowled at the man with the Great Dane puppy, up to his thigh in hedges, and shouted, "Five thirty-seven!" in the same tone she might have shouted, "Get out!"

On the street, people walk by wrapped like packages in coats and scarves, making twisted faces at the weather. The Great Dane puppy pulls his owner down the sidewalk and then stops dead in his tracks, cowering at the wind. Naked trees line the block like rows of skeletons, and Flora pulls a chair up to the window to smoke as the night grows darker, though it's been on the verge of dark since half past four. The cigarettes mark time as she waits for Rock to call her back. She wills him with every exhale to pick up the phone and dial her number, to respond to her comment. "You don't know anything about me!" he might yell. What she would give to hear him yell.

There are voices on the steps as Rock lugs boxes with the new tenants, the wordless buzz cutting through the thick, musty air of the old building. The clunk of the radiator kicking in startles Flora, not because it scares her but because it will continue to clunk this way through winter whether it is happy or not.

Flora retreats to her bed and decides to nap until Rock calls back. Again she dreams she has insomnia. She's dreamed a variation of this dream for weeks now; sleep exhausts her— she never gets any sleep in her sleep. In her dream now, she wanders her apartment, room to room, trailing her quilt behind her like a child. She makes herself warm milk and finishes only half before she puts the mug on the tub's edge, draws a bath, and slides into its heat, letting the washcloth lie across her belly, ears dipping below the surface into watery silence that sounds like the blood rushing through her body. In these dreams Flora knows how to take care of herself; she knows what to do to survive. But always, still, that constant angry buzz—*I drive people away. How to love? How to love?*

"People are just silly," the woman says pertly on her way past Flora's door, and Flora lurches out of the gray weather of sleep. The woman's voice sounds like an effort to be cheerful at the end of hours of moving, with the first night to spend ahead of her in the new apartment stacked with boxes stuffed with things that have lost their meaning moved from their rightful places. Flora imagines the standing lamp in the corner by her door out on the street, unrecognizable. She holds it by its neck for balance as she leans against her door. There is no bump, bump, bump of boxes, so they are finally empty-handed on their way upstairs. *Silly* is a word that means nothing, Flora thinks—like *crazy, nice, weird,* or *interesting.* Flora convinces herself that the woman must be talking about Rock, helping her husband to see that Rock is just a child, not a man who might come between them. She rushes to the hole in her kitchen floor.

Pulse. Rock turns on his TV—a sitcom with canned laughter every third line—to go with his cereal while upstairs in the new tenants' apartment a chair slides across a room, newspaper crackles, a giggle trickles like water through dry stone. The silliness, Flora thinks, fighting back. She puts the phone by the bed in case Rock comes to his senses. She sleeps in the T-shirt she's worn all day, dreams brightly colored flannel pajamas into the back of her dresser drawer. In her dream she pulls warm wool socks up to her knees and walks outside in the snow. The socks are quickly soaked through and the hairy wool clings damply to her calves as she wanders the neighborhood, though even here in her subconscious she is exhausted.

The next day at work, she sits in the tiny back room of the art gallery surrounded by piles and piles of haphazardly stacked art books. The front room of the gallery is just as tiny, filled now with a series of paintings with brightly colored backgrounds—red, orange, pastel blue—each with large overlapping gold rings like the symbol for the Olympics. All the paintings are framed in shiny gold frames. Flora thinks they are hideous. She told her boss, Samson, and he agreed but said, "Flora, sometimes art is hideous. Sometimes art isn't pretty." It's something Samson has been saying since Flora first starting working for him, a refrain that has become sound without meaning. Now Flora stares at the paintings—her scratchy gloves, scratchy hat, scratchy scarf, and scratchy coat piled at her feet—trying to recapture that season when life hid mysteriously around a corner up ahead, mischievous and playful. "Sometimes, Peter, art isn't pretty," she used to say, getting up from the table and slithering around the mostly empty Indian restaurant à la Samson. Peter would have to spit his tandoori chicken into his napkin. She could make him laugh that hard. "Sometimes art is like a pimple—hideous and yet salaciously succulent, on the verge of bursting." She would go on and on.

A man wanders in, looking for warmth. Flora hopes he will linger, but he scans the wall dubiously, not understanding that sometimes things in life that are ugly are actually trying to be beautiful, then pulls his jacket collar up around his ears and heads back out into the night.

No one calls except the collectors or art dealers, who are tired of her excuses. Samson isn't here, she swears. Even when he is here, he tells her to say that he's not. He owes money. Lots and lots of money. He will be back this afternoon, Flora promises, this evening, tomorrow, next week. Would you like to leave a message? Would you like to leave another? Would you like to hold? There is no hold option on this antique phone. There isn't even call waiting. Flora just hangs up. A man in coveralls comes in near the end of the day and without looking at Flora walks up to the biggest, ugliest painting—thousands of those Olympic rings against a washed-out background—and plucks it from the wall.

"Marty sent me," he says. "Smile, it's not so bad."

Flora thought she was smiling.

Flora thinks of the new tenants sorting through boxes, holding items up—"Where should *this* go?"—and making love on their bare, dusty floor because even the dust holds temptation in their new home. She never wanted to marry Peter; she wanted to be his deepest, darkest friend, and when that didn't work out, she headed others off at the pass. But with Rock she feels a connection surging up through the hole in the kitchen floor. She leaves work early, eager to return to her post at the window.

There is a knock on Flora's door just as Flora is speed-dialing Rock's number, and she is furious at whoever it is because she knows it is not he. She can hear him scuffling around his kitchen. Every couple of scuffles she glimpses tufts of his unwashed hair through the hole.

"It's Rock here," his answering machine message says.

There's music in the background—the wail of background singers hitting notes of blissful despair. "You know what to do." The casual indifference of his voice causes Flora to speak in a higher pitch than she'd intended.

"Rock, there is a serious issue that I have to discuss with you. Call me immediately." She hopes that he will hear the intimacy of her not identifying herself, of her assuming that he knows her voice. It pleases her to imagine him trying to ignore her call, walking away from the phone. She has altered his day in some small way.

When Flora flings the door open indignantly, a young, gangly woman bursts into the apartment like a bird that has accidentally flown in the window. She carries two shopping bags with small shovels poking out of the tops.

"I was on my way home from the garden store and I noticed your flower box filled with those dry branches." The young woman is already headed for the window. "And I just thought since I bought extra . . . What are your favorite flowers?" Her voice is chirpy like a bird. Silly, silly, silly. She opens the window and a blast of cold air forces Flora back a few steps, but the young woman is unstoppable. She reaches out and grabs Flora's flower box off the ledge. It is filled with gravelly dirt, dried twigs that have held their own for years, and a small dead mouse. "Oh dear," the young woman says resolutely, picking the mouse up by the tail and heading for Flora's bathroom to flush. "The plumbing's not that strong," Flora says, but the woman is determined. Flush, flush, flush.

"I'm Liza," she says, extending her newly washed hand

but still moving, letting Flora's hand drop in order to reach into her bag. "Your upstairs neighbor."

"Flora," Flora says. She leans against the counter, arms folded, to watch Liza empty the old dirt into the garbage and start anew.

"Bulbs." Liza holds them up like precious eggs. Flora nods helplessly. "You keep them inside."

"I've never once touched that flower box." Flora is stunned at the way Liza just waltzed right in, and also by the fact that it never occurred to her to touch the flower box. "I've lived here five years and I never thought about it once."

"That's what neighbors are for," Liza says primly, choosing to interpret Flora's words as gratitude. "Which window is your favorite view?"

Flora does not answer. Of course it would be this one. Flora feels suddenly possessive of this window, this view that is hers alone. Liza's face reminds Flora of a slim, long dog bone made of rubber—she saw the man with the lurching Great Dane holding one in his gloved hand recently. Her skin is smooth and glossy like that bone. Flora curbs the impulse to touch it.

"Have you ever been bored?" Flora asks, though what she really wants to ask is does Liza smoke. She knows the answer already. Liza has never been still. Even when she sleeps, she must sleep an active sleep, deep and invigorating but always flailing an arm or a leg or planning the next day, planning whole meals during REM, soup to nuts.

"Like wanting something to happen?" Liza digs her hands

up to the wrists into the soil. "I'm always wanting something to happen. So maybe I'm always bored?"

"Do you want a cigarette?" Flora says.

"Oh sure, I love to smoke," she says, like I love sports or I love this or that movie. "I never do around my husband, but I love to whenever I get the chance." Liza gestures to the ceiling and rolls her eyes, indicating her husband's disapproval, and accepts the pack Flora retrieves from the windowsill. "It always looks so good on people. I mean, just look at you. You look like a movie star."

Flora inhales deeply, feeling suddenly and suspiciously fabulous. "You think?"

The phone rings and Flora just shakes her head, stilling her urge to jump for it, and blows a smoke ring. "I screen," she says, though she's never let the phone ring in her life.

She holds herself perfectly still as Rock's voice thuds into the room. "Flora, Rock. I'm dizzy these days, from my head. I'm seeing a doctor, a specialist, about it and then I'll talk to you about your floor. Later."

Flora gestures with her head toward the hole in the kitchen floor the way Liza did to her husband upstairs.

"That's a doozy, Flora," Liza says, getting down on all fours to investigate. She sticks a long, skinny arm into the hole and wiggles her fingers as if she is retrieving something that has fallen in. Flora pictures her heart, still beating in Rock's sink. "What is wrong with that Rock anyway? We can't stand for that," Liza declares. Flora suddenly has visions of a tenants' committee headed by Liza. Bulbs in every apartment! She imagines Liza filling in the hole in her kitchen floor with a homemade concoction she read about in a magazine, made from spackle and gardening dirt.

Flora wants Liza to leave now. She doesn't want to be on Liza's committee; she doesn't like the way Liza assumes something is wrong with Rock or the way she includes Flora in her *we*. Flora is certain that when Liza is through with her, there won't be a thing Liza doesn't know about Flora—her dreams about insomnia, her love for Rock, whether she believes in God. She senses Liza's investigatory powers, the way she scans a room looking for clues.

Liza wanders into the living room, flicks on the TV to a cop show with heart, gunshots, and tender moments. Flora feels defenseless against this long, rubbery-faced woman bouncing around her apartment. A young cop is about to tell his partner a secret that he hasn't even told his wife. Rock watches the same show downstairs, and the drama echoes throughout the building.

"I'll stop by again soon, hon," Liza says, though she is probably ten years younger than Flora. "Gotta cook the old man dinner." She giggles as she says "old man." She is a great appreciator of her own jokes. And suddenly she is gone, leaving Flora with the young cop's secret. He's had headaches, terrible headaches, dizziness, what should he do? He's seeing a doctor, a specialist.

She runs to the hole, cups her hands to her mouth, and screams down at the single tile, "I know your tricks. Don't you try it!" The silence after Rock turns off the TV has a pulse of its own. Now he'll have to turn to her for solace. She will comfort him. He will see himself in her. The pulse grows louder like a heartbeat revived.

Flora climbs into her bed with her clothes on and falls asleep listening to the scraping sound of moving furniture above, waiting patiently. She can't sleep in her dreams again. Instead she wanders down the cold, creaky wooden staircase of her building in bare feet gone numb with chill. It is snowing inside, large flakes falling from the ceiling, and Flora skirts the puddles to knock on Rock's door. Maybe he has some wool socks he can lend her. She needs socks desperately, more than she's needed anything in her life. A wind whips her dream nightgown up around her knees and she clutches at it to make it behave. She knocks and knocks, the large snowflakes wetting her hair and her nose, until finally, from behind Rock's door, she hears the sound of bristles and scrubbing. The banisters are piled with snow, a river of snowy water running down the steps. Suddenly, the door flies open of its own accord to reveal Liza on her hands and knees, scrubbing Rock's floor with a toothbrush. Flora wakes up, choking on snow—she swears flakes fly out of her mouth as she coughs in her pitch-black bedroom.

She stays awake all night—less exhausting than sleep—watching the silhouettes of bare branches shake in the wind, until it begins to snow for real outside. All night she watches large flakes fall quickly past the streetlamps' light until everything is hidden under a perfect blanket of snow. The cars, the garbage cans, their lids blown into the street, an abandoned armchair that somebody put out on the curb yesterday, all the stray trash—discarded blue and white "We are happy to serve you" coffee cups, plastic wrapping, chicken bones that threaten to choke the Great Dane puppy. Her love for Rock is like that, hidden, and she realizes she has to find a way to show him.

In the morning Carol calls, though it's not even a Sunday. "I wanted to make sure that you are warm enough, that your pipes haven't frozen." The pipes froze last year and the year before that, and Flora sees clearly the years stretched out before her. "Keep warm, Flora," Carol says and, having gone above and beyond her duty, hangs up. After years of thinking Carol wretched and meek, a slave to the scripture of the self-help guru, Flora imagines her putting the kettle on the stove for tea and contentedly curling up on a soft couch with a book she has been meaning to read, grateful for the distance between them.

At work Flora can barely sit still, filled with the restless, urgent desire to capture Rock's attention. Samson stops in to pick up his messages. He doesn't seem to care about the missing eyesore. He replaces it with a small painting done all in primary colors—blue, yellow, red—with a tiny piece of newspaper collage. "It's a gouache," he explains to Flora. "Extremely Mondrianesque," he adds in a hushed, important tone.

"Oh, shut up," Flora says, desperate for him to go so she can leave.

"What did you say?" Samson asks. He seems surprised that she talks at all.

"I'll shut up the store," she says.

"Of course you will," Samson says, a look of puzzled bemusement on his face. Flora sees the way he thinks of her, as another museum piece to observe and then sidle away from. He walks out the door backward, like someone robbing the place. "I'm not here," he whispers. "I am a figment of your imagination." "And I am one of yours," she says. He laughs as if this were funny. Flora leaves as soon as Samson rounds the corner, leaving the phone to ring and ring, eager to get home to prove to Rock that she is not a figment of his imagination and to herself that she is not a figment of her own.

On her walk home from the subway, she spots Liza at the counter of the neighborhood video store, her long rubber dog bone face flushed. The clerk behind the counter is ruddy with flirting. He twists a small stud in his ear and looks at Liza sideways. Flora slips inside, slinks down the Foreign Movies section, past the Action/Adventure section to find a suitable place to study Liza.

"This is my favorite customer," the video boy says to the other clerk on duty, a girl with haphazard pigtails and chunky glasses. "And it's only her first time here." The pig-tailed girl rolls her eyes but Liza doesn't notice. She smiles, saying, "You are being so silly." She touches his arm effortlessly as she slides two videos across the counter. There is a sweetness to Liza's gesture that makes her rubber face beautiful, fixed for a moment in coy, rosy bliss. "Look at that," Flora says out loud without even realizing she's speaking. She is that stunned by Liza's easy transformation. Flora feels the chill creeping over her own bones, encasing them like branches in ice. She is fragile and raw like the naked trees on her block. She is paralyzed in the New Releases section in front of a row of movie boxes—with couples on the verge of passion; boxes that depict redemptive love, mysterious loss, and what the world would be like after World War III. As Liza walks out the door under the warm gaze of the video boy, Flora realizes something must be done or her blood will freeze up inside of her, crack her from the inside out.

"You shouldn't flirt like that. It's embarrassing," the pigtailed girl says, elbowing the ruddy boy clerk as he sweeps the drop box with one arm for returned videos. Flora agrees. She feels betrayed, last night's dream lingering like the bitter smell of old cigarette smoke in her apartment. Liza invading her life one day, then flinging her attention in an entirely different direction the next. More than this, she fears Liza will turn her attentions on Rock next. Panicked, she follows Liza tripping lightly down the street toward their brownstone. Flora leans into the wind, filled with a decisiveness that warms her like a pneumatic fever as the winter sky sinks lower.

The daggers of hail ringing in her lungs begin to melt as she reaches the brownstone and lets herself inside, the lock still warm from the turn of Liza's keys before her. Flora takes the stairs two at a time, beelining it for that hole in the kitchen floor. Rock runs water in the sink below to clean his cereal bowl, and Flora feels the hot water rush over her heart lying there in the dirty dishes. As she digs Liza's slick bulbs out of the new earth in the flower box, Flora's face is set in grim determination like the snowman the neighborhood children have made in the street, its mouth made of raisins. As she drops the first bulb through the hole, she imagines a SWAT team busting down Rock's door to retrieve her heart, dry it off, wrap it in a towel, and resuscitate it.

"Hey, what the hell?" Rock shouts as the bulbs bounce against his kitchen floor.

There is a muffled movie scream from upstairs while the voices that are the background of Rock's answering machine message rise up through the floor in ecstatic agony. Flora pours the rich dark earth slowly, as if she were pouring dirt on a coffin.

"Holy shit," Rock sputters. Covered in soil, he looks up finally through the hole, but Flora is gone.

She sits on the edge of her bed, suddenly very tired. She is genuinely tired for the first time in months, so tired she could sleep in her sleep. She looks out the window. The sky has lifted. The night is blue-black and clear, filled with stars.

Tonight I'm a woman who was held captive by a married couple, tied to a chair in their basement for several years. Two or three, I can't remember as I sit in the studio dressing room in front of a mirror framed with big yellow lights. I paint dark circles under my eyes with black face makeup. With this, I achieve the tired, worn, but recovering victim look that the audience craves. They will ask me if the couple tortured me physically. At which point a more daring but still appropriately embarrassed member of the audience will ask me if I was tortured sexually. Sometimes I rehearse these answers and other times I make them up on the spot. The hesitancy in my voice gives me credence. They will ask me whether I learned to love my captors. I loved them, I will say. As you love me, I will think.

Then they will say I am brave, that I've suffered through a lot, that I deserve a good life now. I'll say that I never in a million years thought it could happen to me. I'll dab at my eyes with a handkerchief provided by Perry, the show's handsome host, who occasionally appears in my dreams, all the while thanking the audience for helping me to cry at last. I put on a face of regular tears, which are more palatable than the way the real woman who lost her daughter in a freak blizzard in Florida behaved. After they'd returned from the second commercial break, she began to scream a scream that dogs might hear and then ran offstage to throw up. Some happy medium is what the audience wants. Most don't know that what comes after the initial anguish is something that looks more like boredom than anything else. I look at my own static face in storefront windows on the way to work, yawning restlessly, as if against my will.

As I slip the black, curly wig over my own hair-netted, mousy brown hair, Don, the production assistant, opens the door a crack to cue me. I'm on in five minutes. This is the second year that I've worked as a fill-in for this local TV station on *Do Unto Others*. When the show can't get a real woman who was locked in a one-room shack for ten years with a bucktoothed maniac, they call me. When the woman who has sex with her pet python got the flu, it was me that they called.

Misery has turned out to be a fairly profitable business. I've played a woman who slept with her son, a woman who was raised by wolves, a woman who was enslaved by a religious cult. You name it, it happened to me. To the audience, I'm the genuine dirt, the stuff of back alleys, the blue-black fade of the pictures of missing children. If the pouches under my eyes, built from layers of foundation, are slightly uneven, or a lock of my real hair jumps out from under that day's wig, the audience is willing to overlook it. They chalk it up to the disheveled quality they expect in long-term sufferers.

Don comes back to say that I'm on. As I walk out into the studio lights, headed for the familiar chair next to Perry, I feel the eyes of the audience on my sagging shoulders and my slightly mussed wig hair. They scan my body for invisible scars, battle wounds, anything.

They scoop down into my tainted soul. They rush for the soft spots, seeking out the wounds. As I sit down faux-meekly in the round armchair, I smell the eagerness, and the charge of victimhood zip-zaps through my body. Perry turns to me, smiling, and says softly, so as not to startle me, "Welcome, Leslie."

My name is Rita as I drive home from the studio still in costume. I accidentally sat on the sash of Leslie's denim wraparound skirt getting into the car, and as I drive it pulls the skirt tight, digging into my belly. I told Perry that I thought she should wear a nice dress, something flowery, but he insisted that Leslie hadn't seen the light of day for years.

"This skirt was probably the last thing she looked good in before the married couple put her in their basement," Perry said. Perry gets involved in the characters he creates. "Trust me, she never knew how to dress."

It was a day like any other really. The usual questions. "How long did the married couple keep you in their basement?" "What were their names?" "Did they drive nice cars?" "Did this traumatic experience cause you to gain or lose weight?" There was some confusion when a hefty man with a starched white collar raised his hand and asked whether there had been any sex up the butt. Perry turned to me and said, "Leslie, I know this is painful, but was there any anal sex involved?" I got confused. Between me and the husband or between the husband and the wife? Or did the wife strap on a dildo? I wasn't prepped for this question. "I don't remember," I said, looking straight at this man yearning for something ugly.

I started working for *Do Unto Others* two years ago when my mother died. I called home one day and my father was so confused that when he answered the phone he was panting like a dog. "Rita," he said, "I can't talk right now. Your mother's having a heart attack." When he called back, she was dead.

My father called me a lonely spinster once, and that's how I'd come to think of myself. I used to watch the talk shows just to feel better. When my mother died, I started playing the "Well, at least I'm not . . ." game. Well, at least I'm not being held captive by a married couple. Well, at least I'm not afflicted with a disease that causes me to pick at my face until I am bloody and unrecognizable. I clipped newspaper articles: "Woman Marries Horse: 'He's the Only One Who Really Understands Me,' " "Man Shoots Wife and Family 'Just Because,' " "Ballerina Chews Off Million Dollar Leg in Bear Trap Catastrophe." I imagined that I was the horse bride, the murderous husband, and the ballerina. I imagined I was them just long enough to be truly glad I wasn't when I stopped.

Do Unto Others was looking for a substitute guest at about that time. They'd started to run out of ideas, and they feared that they would soon be taken off the air. Their real guests had become too demanding, complaining incessantly about hotel accommodations, not telling all so as not to give away the end of the TV movie being made about their lives. I brought in my cardboard box full of newspaper clippings, and Perry hired me on the spot. He didn't know that I was already practiced at the art of relieving my grief by putting someone else's on. I had no idea then that it would become my life, that I would be doing it still, two years later, at the age of forty-eight.

I'll admit that at first it was an escape from my mother's death. I left home long before she died, but still, she was my one true friend. "Rita," she would say at some point during our weekly phone conversations, "you are a good woman, a very good woman." When she said this, I imagined that the rest of the world thought this highly of me. Possibilities waited in some other room, in some other house miles away, if only I could get to it. The room was filled with friends and admirers who never watched *Do Unto Others* but would recognize when I arrived that here was a good woman standing before them, one who deserved to feel the warm, gentle pressure of a human hand touching her face.

I keep the envelopes from my mother's letters by my bed. She sprayed them with her perfume, and late at night when I can't sleep I sniff their faded scent. I inhale deeply, recapturing that feeling of hope. When I fall asleep, I sometimes have the dream in which Perry is my plastic surgeon, tenderly handling sections of my face as he sculpts and rearranges.

When my mother died, I realized that all her life she was meant to die. That her death was inevitable seemed like a mean trick, something she and I should have talked about more when she was still alive. I worried too that my father, in his old age, didn't have the mental energy to preserve the details of my mother wholly in his mind. I imagined my mother fading completely from this world and I decided that it was my job to remember her. *Do Unto Others* is more than simple escape, more than the "Well, at least I'm not . . ." game. The show is my way of holding my mother to this earth. When I walk out onto the stage, I am grief personified in a mask turned inside out a million times. I'm a reminder to us all.

· · ·

Over the years, I've learned to jump into grief like a swimming pool. The people I play on *Do Unto Others* have allowed me to swim through wet, sloppy sadness with a suitable stroke, a stroke that the audience recognizes, one that they can imitate.

"I know this isn't anything like being raised by wolves," a woman in a blue polyester pantsuit says during today's show, "but sometimes the way my parents raised me felt, well, wild. Uncivilized."

The members of the audience crane their necks to get a better look, as if finally this woman might provide them with an answer to all the questions in the world.

Perry turns to me, puts a hand on my shoulder. "Well, I'm sure that Shirley can sympathize with you. Can't you, Shirley?" The sound of the audience shifting in their seats is the restless sound of animals about to stampede.

I'm wearing a wolf-brown wig. Faint tufts of facial hair dot my chin and jowls.

"Why yes, I can, Perry," I say. I smile at the woman in the blue polyester pantsuit, and she smiles back. We are lifted momentarily out of that big pool of grief. For a second I suspend her above the child she lost in utero last year, the pending divorce, her daughter who hates her. Well, at least I wasn't raised by wolves, she might be saying. Well, at least I wasn't raised by wolves, I think. We are in this together, and the slope of my mother's forehead drifts back to me, the way it looked when she pulled her hair back on days she couldn't be bothered.

• • •

Today I am Tina, a married woman who is addicted to affairs with married men. I'm feeling a little confused because Perry is a married man, and last night I dreamed that he misplaced my nose during surgery, then pretended not to recognize me without it.

"If I were your husband I'd kill you and then I'd divorce you and then I'd kill the guy you had the affair with," says one man, jumping up from the audience and screaming before Perry gets to him with the microphone.

I tuck a piece of my hussy-red wig behind my ear and smile the smile of someone who believes strongly in her infidelity.

"Let's get this straight," Perry says, pacifying the audience. "You'd kill her and then divorce her." The audience laughs. Perry is on my side. He is here to give my grief away.

"Let's get this straight," Perry says again to focus the audience as he takes his seat next to mine on the stage. "You sleep with married men because this way you have the same amount to lose. It's an exchange of risk and loss, if you will."

"That's right, Perry," I say. "It's a reciprocal relationship."

Then Perry does something he's never done before. He touches me. He puts his hand on my shoulder, letting his fingers slip past where my dress covers my skin. His hand brushes Tina's jugular, burning with its foreign heat her skin so unfamiliar with touch.

He doesn't stop there. He kisses me on the cheek. As it's

happening, I miss the moment already—the soft lips of it, the breath-minty breath of it on my face—already configuring itself in my dream landscape. He kisses me in slow motion and then, bang, back to normal speed, and he's saying what he usually says.

"Thank you for sharing with us, Tina," as if he's never met Rita. This fresh agony snaps me momentarily out of the constant hum of grieving. Then, when Perry gets into his car to drive home after the show, waving good-bye as if it was just another day at work, the hum returns.

My cat ran away when I was seven, and there was a shallow dip of grief. It dipped in and touched my little soul. When my mother died, that grief went through me like a bullet, leaving a clean hole, taking parts of me with it. Then there is this new grief that falls somewhere in between a runaway cat and a dead mother, the minty blue wind of a man who kisses you the way no one has kissed you before, sucking the life out of you with his lips. This is the way it is with Perry.

As I get into my car, I look in the mirror and realize I've forgotten to take off the curly red wig. I toss it onto the passenger seat, reminding myself that I never intended to do this forever. I'm just never sure when sadness will brush past me like some rude stranger.

Years ago, when I still lived with my parents, my mother and I witnessed a car accident. A boy walked away from one of the crumpled cars without a scratch, then the blood came up in staggered waves from his mouth. A police officer who arrived at the scene told us the boy had swallowed part of a windshield. My mother said he would have been better off had he swallowed the whole smooth rectangle of the windshield rather than the tiny splintered shards. That's how I feel about dressing up as these big griefs, pain so unimaginable that it swallows in one gulp the death of my mother, my runaway cat, the touch of Perry's fingers on my neck and nothing more.

I pull into a gas station on the way home, and the attendant studies my face as I tell him to fill it up. On rare occasions, people recognize me from *Do Unto Others*. "Sally, as a fellow woman, I know just what it's like to lose all your teeth at such a young age," a woman once said loudly through loose dentures, down the length of a crowded aisle in a grocery store.

There was one show where I played a woman who was addicted to sadness. A woman in the audience began to talk about her estranged sister, and suddenly an adolescent boy next to her screamed out the name of his best friend who'd moved all the way across the country. When the older man in the back row brought up the fact that his real parents gave him up for adoption, Perry said, "Ladies and gentlemen, let's get back to the subject at hand. The topic of today's show is 'addiction to sadness.' " He paused and looked out into the audience. For the first time in the show's history, he didn't say anything. The sadness was everywhere, floating in midair above us all, cloudy beyond recognition.

So when the gas station attendant bends down next to my window and says, as if there is a secret between us, "Look, I know it sounds like a cheap line, but I'm serious—haven't I seen you before? Your face is so familiar—do you work at the Stop and Shop?" I shake my head no. "I can't put my finger on it, but I know I've seen you," he says, handing me my change. "I'm sure you did," I say reassuringly, and all of us feel the stroke of a smooth, warm hand of comfort.

GENEALOGY

When the phone rang in the middle of the night, Bernard answered it even though he wasn't in his own apartment or even in his own city. It made him feel needed for once.

"What?" he said into the receiver, eyes still closed. He was emerging from the deep fog of postcoital sleep. The woman lying next to him, moist and naked, said something about getting the fucking dog off the bed though there was no dog, then rolled over, pulling the tangle of covers with her.

The person on the other end of the line said nothing. "What?" Bernard asked again, starting to feel a familiar panic—the sensation was one of small birds flying in his chest. For him, middle-of-the-night phone calls meant death (his ex-wife's) or anguish (his daughter's). "Is everything okay?" he said. The tiny frantic wings beat against the cage of his heart.

"Who are you?" a nervous male voice asked.

"Come on," Bernard said. What a question. "Can't you do better than that? Isn't there anything else you'd like to know?" For the past several weeks since taking a leave of absence from the university, Bernard had lived his life like this: he drove rental cars up and down the East Coast, spending nights with women who found his kind of drifting irresistible or else they found him just pathetic enough (finally, a man who needed directions). In the tourist area of rest stops, women asked him if he was lost (*And how!* he always thought). Once, as he wandered through a roadside plastic dinosaur park on Route 1 in Massachusetts, a woman—a paleontologist who took study breaks there—appeared seemingly out of nowhere and asked him if he wanted a tour.

The woman lying next to him had said she smelled his sadness. "What does sadness smell like?" he'd asked. "Maple syrup," she said. He reminded her that he'd been eating pancakes when they first met. "No, *you* smelled like syrup," she insisted. It was his scent that drew her to him as he sat alone in the twenty-four-hour Greek coffee shop underneath her apartment on a grim strip of discount tire stores, electonic stores advertising beepers for sale, nail salons, and across the street, the psychiatric hospital the color of dried blood.

"That fucking dog," the woman said and flipped over, pulling a pillow over her face.

"Look," the nervous voice suddenly burst forth. "I call

this number occasionally to get off. Are you happy now? I pick up the phone and dial randomly, and every once in a while I get lucky. This is one of my lucky numbers, pal."

"Maybe you dialed the wrong number?" Bernard asked.

"It's no wrong number," the nervous voice said defiantly. "I've got it on speed dial."

In the hotels where Bernard stayed, when he wasn't staying with one of these women (they were never looking to take him on permanently—the fact that he was a wanderer was part of his lonely charm), he was treated with the respect due a man in his late fifties with all the nutty professor trappings—shabby tweed coat, unkempt hair and graying beard, the way he smelled of musty, cramped offices piled high with old, decaying books (except when he was having pancakes with maple syrup).

Bella looked out from under her pillow—she was a beauty not everyone could appreciate, with eyes so close together it made people a little cross-eyed to look at her and a crooked Roman nose. "Is that Ralph? Ralph, fuck off, you fuck." She took the phone from Bernard and threw it down, then put her hand over Bernard's, let it linger in a way that made him think of earlier, her soft pubic hair a darker red than her hair, against his face. He reached over to touch her, and she reached just beyond him to pull a condom from the box on the bedside table, handing it to him as she closed her eyes and turned her back to him.

"I like to pretend I'm asleep," she said. She was an actress, so Bernard didn't ask.

When the phone began its off-the-hook beeping, Bernard thought: Exactly. Sex is an emergency. For Ralph, for Bella, for me. He sometimes thought of his penis as a surgeon's instrument. Entering somebody else's body in such a profound way must leave a person changed or more knowledgeable. Here's the part where you're full of shit, he heard his ex-wife say. But touching someone else was the only way he kept from floating away these days. Here's the part where you have an epiphany about your life, his ex-wife would have said. Here's the part where you look at the wreckage of your life and make something good out of it. She had always hated to watch him wander aimlessly, something she never did. She had been a big narrator of life as it happened. Her life was a movie, and she was the annoying person in the audience who had seen it before.

The phone rang again, and Bernard pulled out of Bella, still pretending to sleep.

Bella turned and looked at him incredulously. "That's my phone, you know."

"Yes?" Bernard had heard his ex-wife's voice so clearly that he expected it to be her on the phone, telling him to leave his daughter's city if he couldn't bring himself to visit her. Even though Bernard and his ex-wife could barely be in the same room together when she was alive, he'd always taken comfort in the idea of her out there in the world.

"Ah, man," the man said. "Fuck."

"Why'd you call back, Ralph?" Usually people wanted to tell him their sad stories. They hurled them at him like stones from the sinking ships of their lives. After less than twenty-four hours with Bella, she had told him about her wicked parents, her almost-marriage, and the miscarriage that kept her in bed with the shades drawn most days, leaving her apartment only to go to the acting class that she hoped would someday change her life.

"Why don't you shut up, you big fat asshole. My name's not even Ralph."

Here's the part of my life where I get divorced, Bernard's ex-wife had said. Here's the part where I get remarried. And when she died a month ago in a freak avalanche on a ski vacation with her new husband in Italy, she probably thought: Here's the part of my life where I die a ridiculous, accidental death.

"Don't call me an asshole." Bernard hung up the phone and walked through the unfamiliar bedroom in the dark, picking up his clothes on his way to the bathroom. He pulled on his underwear until he realized it was not his but Bella's. He turned on the bathroom light and looked at himself, a grown man stuffed into women's underpants. He had become the person other people thought he was. It was his chairman who had suggested Bernard take a leave of absence after the so-called series of events. Allegedly Bernard had flown several paper airplanes during a seminar he co-taught with another professor—a tiny man, hunched like a comma and squinty from too much time spent reading in poorly lit rooms. Bernard remembered the discussion of the *Oresteia*—but he had no recollection of folding or throwing the airplanes. A student told him later that he'd made a crashing sound as the airplanes hit the walls and fell to the floor. Bernard did remember the day he was attempting to teach Saint Augustine's *City of God* and he'd fallen out of his chair, unable to keep his balance. He'd excused himself to go lie on the cool tile of the men's bathroom, where he was discovered half an hour later by the chairman himself.

The tomato incident occurred soon after. During a meeting with an advisee—another underappreciated beauty with buckteeth and a deliciously raucous laugh—he'd shared fresh tomatoes from his garden. They'd eaten them like apples—the way that he and his once-upon-a-time family had in a house long gone, a house that was still the setting for many of his dreams—the juice dribbling down their chins. There were no napkins handy, and Bernard had started to feel dizzy again, as if he might fall out of yet another chair, so he had leaned over and licked the juice from the student's face. She seemed flattered by this tender gesture. It was a moment of pure physical connection in a world that had started to feel more and more to Bernard like a place without gravity—but the department secretary had walked in, alarmed. The chairman—a man who had recently been charged with sexual harassment—was happy to ignore Bernard lying on the bathroom floor in the face of something he could understand. He clapped Bernard on the back. "A little R and R will do you good," he said knowingly. Bernard hadn't told anyone that his ex-wife had died, that he had only recently become an exwidower. Not even their daughter knew—why would she? He hadn't seen her in years.

Bernard walked back into the bedroom, still in Bella's underwear. Bella was standing in the middle of the room fully dressed, her red hair tied in a knot.

"Cute," she said. "I'm hungry."

In the coffee shop they sat in a booth next to two men drinking coffee and eating baklava. "I don't want to talk about the Knicks," one of them said. "They're not talking about me."

Bernard and Bella ordered coffee and rice pudding.

"Before it comes," Bella said, "let's try something."

Out the window Bernard could see the hospital. "Whatever," he said.

"Don't be such a fuck-and-run type," Bella said. "Humor me a little."

"All right, all right," Bernard said, and he touched her crooked nose. Here's the part where I marry you, his ex-wife had said. Here's the part where we have a beautiful child filled with the potential of all children who have not lived long in the world. Here's the part where our child drops out of college and moves from city to city. Here's the part where our child presses her tender, pulsing veins against my ear to let me hear the blood swirl and rush, begging to be let out. Here's the part where I tell her it's supposed to rush and swirl, but she says no, her blood is filling the rooms of her apartment, sloshing against the walls, rushing to drown her.

"Imagine the weight of the mug, the smell of the coffee, the bitter taste," Bella said.

"But my real coffee is on the way," Bernard protested. The waitress sloshed two cups of coffee in front of them. "In fact," Bernard said, "here it is." He reached for the cream, but Bella swatted his hand away.

"Use your imagination," Bella said, retying the knot in her hair.

"Imagination was never my strong suit." Bernard lifted his cup into the air between them, as if she wouldn't be able to see it otherwise.

"Aren't you an English professor?"

"Western Civ," Bernard said. "*Was.*"

"Give a girl a break," Bella said. She lifted the cup out of his hands and put it on the table. "If you'd just focus."

Here's the part where our child moves from hospital to hospital. Here's the part of my life where I have to rally alone again, his ex-wife had said. Here's the part of your life where you have to get off your sorry ass and rally, she told Bernard, but he couldn't. He'd never set foot in any of the hospitals. Sitting here across the street from the dried-blood building where his daughter was now was as close as he'd ever gotten. There were the middle-of-the-night calls from various cities over the years: Are you really my father? What did you do with my father? Who are you really?

Was it possible he felt too much, that if he saw his daughter with her swirling, rushing blood in the hospital that the tiny birds would beat their way out of his heart? You're such an asshole, he heard his ex-wife say. There are parts you are leaving out. There are parts of you in her, your blood rushing and swirling in her veins. It was true, Bernard had longed to press the tender, pulsing veins of his own wrist to someone's ear, to anyone's ear; he'd pressed his wrist to Bella's ear last night, but she didn't wake up, which seemed to him a good sign, a sign that his blood was not yet clamoring to be let out, because this is what he was most afraid of—the possibility that he'd inherited in reverse this rushing and swirling from his daughter.

"I'm focusing," Bernard said. "I'm focusing."

"I'm telling you, nerve tissue remembers things." She pressed a hand over Bernard's eyes, and though he tried to think of coffee cups, any coffee cup, all the coffee cups he had ever lifted to his lips, there she was—his daughter at his door several years ago, on a day pass, or maybe she'd broken out again, he hadn't asked. It was the first time he'd seen her in years, though his ex-wife had pleaded in between bouts of ignoring him. His daughter pressed her hands over his eyes. Guess who? The gesture in reverse, all things in reverse, everything flowing backward. Taking her hand away, she moved closer to him as if she were about to ask him to dance, not like someone who wanted to dance but like someone who wanted to get inside of him. When she kissed him, her tongue was like a surgeon's instrument claiming his body for her own, seeking out the disease.

"Can you feel it? The weight of the cup in your hand?" Bella asked.

"Yes," Bernard said, opening his eyes, filling them with the flesh of Bella's hand.

"Where are you really?"

"Here," he said, wishing that it were ever true. "Right here."

Mᴀʏʙᴇ it's the other way around? Every unhappy person should have someone happy tapping at their door with a hammer?" Theresa's book group was reading Chekhov this month. She'd recently joined the group after quitting her acting class—she had enough drama in her life with her ex-husband, Richmond, she told Josephine. Plus, she was a set designer. That's where her true talents were, she explained at length. "There are some people who are meant to be behind the scenes. That's me," she said the way she said most things—as if it were a revelation.

Josephine wasn't paying attention today either. She tended to drift off when Theresa got going—the book group fueled Theresa's tendency to philosophize—but today Josephine was particularly distracted. On the radio this morning she'd heard a story about twenty-five million Hindus in Allahabad, India, bathing in holy waters at the confluence of the Ganges and the Yamuna. Naked mystics, bodies anointed with ceremonial ash, leading the way to the plunge into the river in the name of everlasting life in order to be free from the endless cycle of birth and death and rebirth. This seemed especially significant because tomorrow was her birthday, which reminded her of her mother. Tomorrow she would turn the age her mother was when she retreated to her bedroom and never came out again.

Even more immediately alarming had been the little specks like tiny spiders that danced their way across Josephine's vision as she listened to the story about the plunging mystics. They were there when she first woke up, but she dismissed them as a sign that she desperately needed coffee. Now she closed her eyes and opened them again to see if the spiders would go away, but there they were. As the spiders twirled and dipped, she watched the two girls who lived across the street play with a car battery tossed out on their front lawn. The battery looked as if it had narrowly escaped a fire, its edges singed. Josephine blinked again, but the spiders still hovered.

A man pushed a pile of mattresses stacked on a rolling cart down the street. On top of the pile of mattresses was another man sleeping under a blanket. At the end of the street were mysterious piles of wood, like something about to be rebuilt. The neighborhood was filled with things that needed to be repaired but never would be.

"And *this* is the city named one of the ten best small cities if you don't want to live in New York?" Theresa asked, gesturing to the sleeping man rolling down the street.

"I think I'm going blind," Josephine said, so softly that Theresa didn't hear her.

Theresa blew on her coffee to cool it, and even though it was a beautiful day and their chairs were turned to catch the sun the way they'd set them up every morning since the weather turned warm, this struck Josephine as an especially useless gesture. She wanted to shake Theresa and tell her that.

"Are you even listening to me?" Theresa asked.

Josephine started to apologize, but there were the spiders. They retreated a little, flickering at the edges of her vision.

"I'm not feeling very well," she said, louder this time.

"It's practically your birthday," Theresa said, blowing on her coffee again. "You've got birthday nerves."

"Just let it sit. The air will cool it." Josephine took the coffee out of Theresa's hands and put it on the ground.

"That's dangerous, you know," Theresa called out to the girls playing with the battery. The girls looked up blankly, as if that was the point, then banged on the battery with a rock. Josephine couldn't agree more.

"Shouldn't those kids be in school?" Theresa looked at the wristwatch her ex-husband, Richmond, had given to her, as if knowing the time would provide an answer to her question.

The man pushing the mattresses lifted the lids of trash containers placed in the street for pickup. Josephine had seen this man before, without the mattresses, looking in the containers just after the garbage man had emptied them. Today the man's disappointment was a sound, a keening that sliced through Josephine like a sharp wind. Is this how it began with her mother?

"But really, don't you think that could be my life soon—joy flickering on the edge of misery? Maybe tonight is about offering me a little joy for once," Theresa said. She picked up her coffee and started to blow a ripple across the surface again.

"Maybe. Just be careful." Josephine said this not so much because she thought Theresa might follow her advice when she saw her ex-husband as because she felt obliged to say it, particularly since she had run into Richmond at the diner around the corner yesterday. It was the first time they'd ever met. She'd been reading alone at a table when he walked in. "Aren't you Theresa's neighbor?" he asked. "The therapist, right?" He joined her for coffee, and though Josephine told herself she was doing it for Theresa's sake (she had even suggested counseling when he said that he and Theresa were having "problems, nothing major"—he was only telling her this because he knew she was a "professional"), she still recalled Richmond's musky aftershave smell and the way he touched her arm when he got up to leave, causing her stomach to drop with desire. What was happening to her? She was going on ten years in this line of work, that must be it. Eli, her terrifically flawless boyfriend, was right, though she would never admit it to him; she needed a break. Was she telling herself to be careful more than she was telling Theresa? She felt bad for letting her impatience intrude on this friendship, and for having coffee with Richmond and not telling Theresa, so she squeezed Theresa's shoulder.

"Don't be such a worrier," Theresa said, shrugging her off, alarmed by this uncharacteristic display of affection. "I'm not your client."

But that's how their friendship had started three months ago, the night Theresa first moved in. Theresa banging on her door in the middle of the night; Josephine letting her in—"We could see about getting you a bed at a shelter" and then "Why don't you sleep here on the couch." Richmond had threatened her with a knife. "He never uses it; it's a prop. It's a bread knife. It's serrated, for god's sake," Theresa said.

It was never clear to Josephine how much of what Theresa told her was for effect. She was always taking things back, or adjusting them after she succeeded in shocking Josephine initially. Like the time Theresa said she suspected Richmond had secretly killed his own dog so that Theresa would think his dog died naturally and feel sorry for him. The next day she retold the story so that Richmond had put the dog out of his misery because he was old and sick. Whether Theresa was telling the truth or simply trying to restore order didn't seem to make a difference. Either way it was about taking the world by the throat. Theresa pushed her voice and her body against life in an effort to leave an imprint. Her relationship with Richmond revolved around the drama of their bodies as much as their minds—sex and the potential for violence intertwined. "Sex was best after a fight," Theresa told Josephine yesterday over coffee. "At least we put our hostility to good use."

That first night, Theresa fell asleep sitting up on Josephine's couch, her tea balanced perfectly in her lap. Josephine watched her and was suddenly willing to throw all her training as a social worker out the window for the possibility of having her own friend—someone apart from colleagues or Eli's friends. She and Eli had moved to this town a year ago because Eli had gotten a position at the university teaching psychology. Josephine had difficulty making friends, and here was someone who lived right next door, and—she hated to admit this part—someone whose fucked-up life might distract her from the feeling that had started as a seed a year ago and grown and grown, headed for today, the feeling that there was a genetic tidal wave coming her way, that there was no escaping from the undertowlike sorrow that had waited all her life to drag her out to sea. But that was ridiculous, her own hyperbolic nature. It was as ridiculous as reading into the spiders dancing across her eyes, believing they were a wake-up call. And still, they danced. *Get ready*.

"What is going on with you today?" Theresa waved a hand in front of Josephine's face and Josephine batted it out of the way. "You're starting to freak me out."

"I'm sorry. I'm tired—weird dreams. I'm out of it." She waved a hand dismissively in front of her face. The spiders were doing a polka on her eyeballs. "I should really get going."

"I wish I had a broken leg so I could have a cast," one of the girls across the street said to the other. They were sitting in the dirt now, rebuilding the pile they'd just kicked over. "We could draw on it with Magic Markers and people would sign their names and draw hearts on it."

"I wish I was in a wheelchair," the other girl said. "Like, just for a week or a month." She cupped a handful of dirt, letting it pass through her fingers like a sieve.

"What if you were paralyzed from the waist down?" one girl asked, arranging the other girl's hair in a ponytail. "What if you were paralyzed all over?" the other girl asked back. The high thin pitch of their voices was the music of Josephine's soul.

"How's Eli's father?" Theresa asked. "Eli is such a wonderful guy. You're lucky."

"His father is much better," Josephine said. Eli's father lived alone out west and a week ago had fallen down the stairs. Eli had gone to stay with him, though he felt awful about missing Josephine's birthday. "Eli's a wonderful guy," Josephine said. And he *was*—a wonderful, attentive, devoted son and a wonderful, attentive, devoted boyfriend after almost eight years. "I am lucky," she said, reminding herself out loud.

"I'll make sure you have a terrific birthday," Theresa said. "Richmond and I throw great parties."

That's what Josephine was afraid of. She couldn't think of anything worse than a house filled with relative strangers, one of whom might or might not be wielding a knife, serrated or not. But Theresa was a big believer in quantity over quality. She'd insisted on the party.

"Don't go too wild," Josephine said. "It's not as though I'm turning a significant age. I'm fortysomething, remember?"

"All the more reason," Theresa declared, as if that were that.

The girls across the street, with their flat chests and legs too long for the rest of their still-growing bodies, kneeled on their knobby knees to build another pile of dirt. They kicked this one over too, as though, even years from now, that would be all that mattered. They reached down and touched the stone in their walkway. "For good luck," the one girl said to the other, and they seemed charmed, filled with good luck that would let them lead wild, uncharted lives.

"Where are their parents?" Theresa asked. "They should really be in school."

"I think it's a holiday," Josephine said, having no idea whether or not that was true.

"Knock, knock," Theresa said.

"Who's there?"

"Happiness."

Get ready. The spiders jumped for joy.

"I've got to go," Josephine said.

If Eli had been there, he would have told her to take the day off, but Josephine couldn't sit home all day alone with herself.

Her mother hadn't so much died as faded into the sheets. But Josephine had made a career out of the belief that the choices people made changed their lives, prevented them from making the same mistakes their parents made.

So she would go to Christine's house, though Christine was no longer her client. Christine was a resident in one of the shelters where Josephine had worked when she first came to town. Josephine had been in private practice for several months, now in an office she shared with an acupuncturist, but she had recently read an article about a doctor in Haiti who tracked down patients with AIDS who couldn't make it to the clinic for their meds, hiking out into the mountains to make sure they received the doses they needed. Josephine would go to Christine's house and check her refrigerator to make sure there was enough food for the kids, confirm that her murdering ex-husband was no longer living with the family he longed to murder, prevent whatever little she could prevent. Or was it that Christine comforted her, helped her feel her own life more acutely? Josephine was suspicious of herself; she told no one that she went to see Christine, not even Eli, partly because it was highly unprofessional and partly because she wanted the visits to be hers alone. Christine and her two boys made Josephine think of an abrasion where there was no skin at all. That struck Josephine as better than feeling nothing.

When she arrived, Josephine pounded on the door because Christine was deaf in one ear, a broken eardrum from her recent boyfriend, James. The TV was turned up as loud as it could go. Joe, Christine's youngest boy, appeared in the doorway with a fistful of uncapped thick felt-tip markers that smelled like twisted versions of their colors—sweet grape for purple, chemical-apple for green, fading-cinnamon for brown. The dog, Stan, was at Joe's side, the boil on his stomach skimming the ground.

"I was so happy then," Josephine's mother had said to her once, referring to an unspecified time long ago. She said this as she lay in bed wasting away, refusing to eat even broth. Was *now* the happy part of Josephine's life, or was she living the mythic *then*?

She walked into the empty living room and turned off the TV just as Christine emerged from the kitchen, waving hello with a splinted finger.

"James?" Josephine asked loudly.

Christine didn't answer and went to the refrigerator. She returned with two glasses of iced tea, holding her splinted finger out daintily from the glass, a tea party for invalids. "You can't know everything about someone," Christine said. "Even someone steady." Christine nudged a red dump truck out of her path with her toe. "Especially someone steady."

Josephine wanted to protest, to say that James was anything but steady, but that seemed to be what Christine was really saying anyway.

"You could move into the shelter for a while," Josephine said instead. She was sick of herself; she could barely stand the sound of her own voice. Didn't she have anything more insightful to offer, anything more complex? Christine ignored her again and sat down on the couch, handing Josephine a glass clinking with ice.

Joe raised the uncapped markers above his head, walking toward his mother. She uncurled his fingers, prying the markers from his hands and shoving them under the couch, rolling her eyes as Joe fell to his knees to pull out large tumbleweeds of dust.

"Their father is supposed to pick them up in a few days, take them for a while," Christine said. She brushed the bangs from her face with her splinted finger, revealing the scar from where the boys' father, who was not James, had cut her with his other girlfriend's switchblade. She fingered the indentation. " 'My body is marked by the men I've known. It's a calendar of bad love that tells me nothing.' I heard that song on the radio this morning." Josephine studied Christine's cheeks as she spoke, slabs of tender meat.

Josephine felt a sudden urge to ask if she could move in with Christine, sleep on the dusty couch, eliminate the differences between them altogether.

"What can I do to help you?" Josephine asked, meaning the exact opposite.

Christine pulled a clump of dust and hair from Joe's hand. Stan sniffed the clump where it fell, then fell over on his side, his boil hanging loose with fluid, pregnant with possibility.

"Look," Christine said. "I appreciate you coming by. I do." She held her hands in front of her as if she were holding a steering wheel, her splinted finger sticking up like a stiff ghost. "I've got my brother in Florida," she said. Whenever

Christine mentioned her brother in Florida, she pretended she was driving his imaginary car and the conversation was over.

"Christine," Josephine said. She spoke before she realized that her words were more than thought. "I think I'm going blind."

Christine looked up wearily. She reached the hand with the broken finger over to rub Joe's back awkwardly.

"Never mind," Josephine said.

"At least it's only one finger," Christine said firmly. The adhesive tape of the splint scratched up and down Joe's sweater, snagged, and moved on.

Josephine's shoulders stiffened with embarrassment. She'd wanted Christine to jump up from the couch in horror, fluff the couch pillows for Josephine to lay her head. "Blind?!" The blood rushed to her face, heating it up from the inside out.

Josephine was nothing like that doctor in Haiti—she wandered out into the squashed-down world looking for comfort from the people she should be comforting. Christine flipped her arm over to scratch her wrist with the splint and Josephine had a sudden murderous impulse to cut the wrist Christine offered up, to see real blood. She shook her head to empty her mind of the image. She would go home and call Eli. He would straighten her out. "Pull the shades, Jo," he'd say. "Make a cup of tea. Take a nap. Be kind to yourself."

Last night Josephine had found brief comfort on a late-night public TV talk show. A guest scientist had warned against the dangers of bowing down to genetic determinism. And yet all this talk about genomes—how could they not, in addition to everything else, dictate human behavior? That's what the talk show host had said, striking a thoughtful pose, hand on his chin as if he were in the midst of discovering something himself. The trick, Josephine thought, was to arm yourself with your own life philosophies, to learn to tell your own narrative in a way that allowed you to influence your own evolutionary path. *My mother lost her mind so I didn't have to. The fact that I'm aware of the danger makes it that much more preventable. Yeah, my father left—it made me strong, independent, self-sufficient. No, I didn't feel abandoned, actually.* She had these conversations frequently with imaginary dissenters, who often took the form of the late-night talk show host. He'd ask challenging questions, that hand on his chin. *But Josephine, you've had moments where you too wanted to retreat to your bed. Long naps in the afternoon, yes? Your work—is it guilt that motivates you? And how about this Eli? He has made it clear that he loves you, and yet you refuse to even discuss the possibility of mar-riage. What is this about? Perhaps you are afraid you will drive him away the way your mother did your father?* Oh, shut up, she told herself.

"Call me if you need anything," Josephine said to Chris-tine, knowing Christine never would. Then she had an inspi-ration. She wrote her home phone number on a piece of paper and slipped it into Christine's good hand.

"What's this?" Christine asked.

"My home number."

"Am I supposed to be grateful?"

Get set, the spiders whispered.

• • •

Back at her office, Josephine took herself to task for giving a client her home phone number. She shouldn't foster dependency. She'd gone to social work school after her mother died to be able to give something to people who wanted to receive it. At first that provided a joyous, mind-expanding satisfaction, which then became more of a cleaning-the-house kind of satisfaction. Clean laundry folded neatly in drawers; kitchen counter wiped clean; a bathroom that smelled of fake-smelling flowery disinfectant; groceries unpacked, refrigerator arranged so that the levels of food made sense, cans carefully stacked in the cupboard. A now-that's-done kind of satisfaction. She knew she'd shut herself down, wrapped herself in the snappy maxims she offered the women she counseled—"Take care of yourself; no one else will," or "You can't undo your past." It kept their sadness from seeping through. Now that felt wrong—she should feel some of that pain. This talk with herself wasn't having the desired effect.

She thought about calling Eli, then decided against it. His kindness infuriated her. "You need a break," he'd say as he often did, level-headed and calm. His solutions infuriated her.

"You'll be like this someday, no matter how hard you try," her mother had said to her, always quietly (so much better when she screeched), after her father fled. This was before her mother stopped leaving the house altogether, when she still faked fainting spells in movie theaters. Josephine would throw down her popcorn to come to her rescue. That's what she wanted, wasn't it? Or was it? Kindness infuriated her too, and solutions enraged her. In a train station once, she thought she was going deaf because the clerk behind the counter began to speak as a train pulled into a station. Josephine, excited by how easy this round of reassurance would be, pointed to the train, something tangible, something right there in front of them. She laughed with relief.

"You think this is funny?" her mother had said. "I'm in pain here."

"I know that," she said. "I know."

"I wish I would go deaf so you could see the thing devouring me from inside."

"That's a horrible thing to say," Josephine said, packing her bags in her mind. "Never think it again or it might come true."

"I wish it would," she said, and Josephine unpacked her mental luggage once more, feeling the inevitable tug of guilt in the blood they shared.

Josephine canceled her next appointment and went home, where she lay down on her bed. She fell asleep and had a dream in which she walked around and around her own squat house, crowded together among the other one-story houses in the neighborhood for protection, plucking bits of flaking paint to reveal a different color underneath. As she walked, she realized she couldn't remember what day it was, whether it was yesterday or today or tomorrow or next year.

"It's Wednesday," the two girls who lived across the street told her, running through her dream. She woke up, frightened by the blur of her days. She opened her bedroom closet, where her clothes hung like molted skins. There were no groceries, nothing to eat for dinner. This fact pleased her. Over the hum of the refrigerator she listened with satisfaction to the rumbling of her stomach. She thought of the tin cans—peas, corn, beans—in the cabinet, in front of other, dusty cans of hominy, beets, things that sat untouched for years, good ideas at the time. She went into the kitchen and put them in a paper bag. She would take them to the emergency food pantry. It was time to admit she would never, in the entire rest of her life, eat them. She put the paper bag on the kitchen floor, then lay down beside it on the cold linoleum until she could feel darkness surround the house.

She smelled Richmond before she heard him—that musky smell, a parody of what a man should be. He didn't knock. He pushed open the door, which she'd forgotten to lock in her haste to get inside, away from the world. Nothing happens by accident, she remembered telling Christine last week. He walked into the kitchen and found her there on the floor.

"Theresa's not home yet," he said.

Josephine started to get up, and then the same part of her that had wanted to see Christine's blood decided against it. "She's been working late these days."

"I know," Richmond said, and lay down beside her. Josephine had crawled into bed with her mother once. She had too much to drink one night and slipped in beside her after she'd finally fallen asleep. Her mother's body stiffened like a rod as soon as Josephine lay down, but Josephine persevered. She put an arm around that rod and kept it there all night.

Richmond's body was not stiff. It was supple and warm, and as he undressed her, Josephine thought that maybe it wasn't happiness that needed to knock on the doors of the unhappy. Maybe it was other people's unhappiness that needed to knock, or rather, just let itself in. As Richmond's body covered hers, his unhappiness covered hers until there was nothing but heat and movement. And when he left her there, on the kitchen floor, his unhappiness still hovered over her like a blanket.

When Josephine woke up the next morning, she was still lying on the kitchen floor. Richmond had thrown a blanket over her naked body. She was having the inevitable birthday meltdown, she told herself. People should be required to stay home on their birthdays, and on the days surrounding their birthdays. There should be a special padded cell where people could stay until the week of their birth was over. She checked herself for regret, for guilt, for feelings of pain for Theresa, but there were none, at least none that she could feel, which seemed like a really bad sign. At least she wasn't in her bed. That was something to be grateful for.

The phone rang and rang. She let it ring. The answering machine picked up and it was Eli. "Happy birthday, Jo," he said cautiously. "Are you there?"

She could almost say in truth that she wasn't. He worried for her, and she hated to make him worry, but it was as if she gave off a worry-for-me scent. When they first met, she told him the story of her family and he told her the story of his. That was early on when everything, including the idea of the other person heartbroken in some distant past, fueled their attraction for each other. His story was equally full of drama—divorce, affairs, the death of his mother when he was seven. "You're not alone," he'd whispered to her more than once. Somehow, this was never as comforting as it was meant to be.

"I'll call back later," he said. "Hope you're taking the day off and treating yourself."

She couldn't answer the phone, but she would go to the eye doctor. The spiders were back, two-stepping across her vision.

Dr. Piazza, the optometrist, put Josephine's face in a viselike contraption to keep her head still. He adjusted his own thick-lensed glasses, then pressed a button, setting the machine in motion.

As the light came toward her eye, she willed it to blind her. Maimed, she would be excused from any other affliction. She'd strike a deal with the universe—take her sight, she'd take happiness. Happiness might be asking too much—occasional contentment? That seemed reasonable, though she knew it didn't work that way. Through her job, she'd met men and women whose houses had burned to the ground while they were in the hospital on the verge of death, their child on life support in the next room. There was no quota on misery.

The black dots seemed larger now, two ill-fitting eye patches. They breathed, breathing themselves larger and smaller. The machine touched her eye with its round, cold surface. It clung like a plunger and Josephine thought for a minute it would pull her eye entirely out of its socket. She leaned into it to help it along, but Dr. Piazza pulled her head gently back.

"Just relax," he said.

"Floaters," he announced, after the tests. "They're a sign of nearsightedness—remnants of an artery that nourished your eye while you were still in your mother's womb." Josephine was amazed at the prospect of receiving something nourishing from her mother, all these years after her death.

"Sometimes these things resolve themselves," Dr. Piazza said, taking off his glasses to rub his eyes. "The body just takes care of it. We'll wait and see, all righty?"

"All righty," Josephine repeated. She liked the idea of her body as a self-maintaining container for her thoughts, carrying them from place to place like a bucket filled to the brim with sloshing, precious water.

Dr. Piazza recommended she go home—Rest, *take the day off, treat yourself, it's your birthday?! Forget about it! Order in or get your boyfriend—you've got a boyfriend, right? A pretty woman like you? Get that boyfriend of yours to cook you a nice home-cooked meal*—but she decided to make an effort, to make a show of participation in this whole party concept. Something festive—balloons? What was so festive about blown-up rubber? Maybe a colorful assortment of finger foods—vegetables, fruit? Gourds? What *were* gourds anyway?

She made her way carefully to the grocery store, got a cart, and found herself in the fruit and vegetable aisle. And then there she was, on the floor again. She got up from where she'd fallen to one knee, her fingers pressing lightly at her eye sockets. The shadows pulsed in an almost celebratory way, revived, and her life lurched forward like her grocery cart rolling away in zigzags on faulty wheels.

There was something joyful, giddy even, about the dancing spiders this time. They didn't impair her sight so much as focus it. They were nourishment after all. Beyond their wiggling black bodies, Josephine caught a glimpse of melons like giant baby heads, graceful sweeps of green-purple rhubarb stalks, white onions the color of someone's pale skin.

The floaters pulsed like a beating heart and Josephine stroked a melon for reassurance. She felt a surge of excitement like the one she had felt in her dream last night watching the next-door girls run through her house. "Wednesday!" they'd shouted. Today was Friday. The excitement was more vivid than life, but real and really hers.

A rail-thin grocery clerk in a loose green apron pushed Josephine's cart over from where it had rolled into a display of generic green plants, their leaves edged with brown.

"Is this yours?" he asked. He reached a bony arm into the cart and pulled out a carton of milk. He held it up to her as if this would help her decide. Josephine returned the melon carefully to its place, rubbed her eyes with fingers ripe with faint sweet-melon scent.

"No," she said definitively, looking at the grocery cart filled with brightly colored, warty gourds and packages of balloons. Like the Hindu mystics, she must break the cycle. "I don't know whose that is," she said. She noticed the clerk's jagged edges, the sharp outline of his white teeth, and the dent in his apron where his hip bone pressed against it.

"Really," he said. It wasn't a question. He lifted the milk carton into the air in front of Josephine's face. He tapped a long finger against the place where it said *homogenized*.

"Really," she said. She smiled at him to seal the deal. She slid away, her fingers gliding along the sticky metal sides of fruit stands and bread tables; she inhaled the chemical sweet smell of the cakes in the bakery; aware of the track light ticking overhead as she moved past other shoppers pushing their carts. She thrilled at the idea of her cart abandoned.

She would call a cab and leave her car in the grocery store

parking lot, come back for it later. Maybe she would never come back for it. Maybe she was through with that car.

She leafed through the yellow pages and dialed the number of a cab company called At Your Service. It amazed her that cabs would pick you up and take you anywhere you wanted to go, no questions asked. She was no fool; she was a therapist, for Christ's sake. She knew she was on the run, but still she could go anywhere, anywhere at all, and her stomach dropped with the sheer possibility of it. She went outside to wait.

The cabdriver who pulled up in front of the grocery store was a woman with no right forearm who wore a wristwatch on that elbow. This struck Josephine as a brave gesture, and she sank comfortably into the the smoky, plastic smell of the backseat. She closed her eyes, and the black dots became shadows again.

"Going home?" the driver said. She made it sound like a forgotten place, somewhere long abandoned. The driver was older than Josephine, with thick black hair whose curls obscured her face. A black spider, or was it a baby octopus— all those legs—did a jig across Josephine's vision: *Look at me!* She pictured the cab driver at home, chopping carrots with her one good arm on a chopping block, the knob of her slender elbow bobbing up and down with the quick movement, her short, careful nose, deliberate on her otherwise round and sprawling face. She wanted to ask the woman, "What were you making? What did you do with all those carrots?" But when she looked at the picture of the driver on the copy of her driver's license taped to the back of the front seat, she saw a face pained with angles.

Still, Josephine felt it strongly, this memory that didn't belong to her. Was it a memory of her mother? Josephine had moved on with her life in the ten years since her mother's death—crossed state borders, found a satisfying career that put her experiences with misery to good use. She hadn't run away—she'd grown up, grown older. And yet she'd gone nowhere. Here she was, a grown woman in the back of a cab, longing for the time her mother took her camping as a child, on a beach thousands of miles away from where she was now. Memory was a cruel thing. Her mother had found driftwood and seaweed to build a fire on the sand, under the white light of a full moon. She remembered the pine needles between her toes once she took off her shoes. Her mother said they should feel the earth directly. They ate rosehips for dinner, picked them off bushes and held as many as they could in their hands. Mouths full of seeds, they nibbled around the taut skin. The waves threatened to steal them away in the night where they slept on the beach huddled together on a single blanket her mother took off the bed on the way out.

"This you?" the driver asked.

"Yes, it's me," Josephine said though her neighborhood was for a moment unrecognizable. Josephine thought of her car still sitting in the grocery store parking lot. When she got out of the cab, the little girls across the street were sitting on their crumbling stone wall.

"What if I was born in a different family and you weren't

my sister?" one said to the other, who burst into tears and ran inside.

"What a baby," the first girl said out loud, for Josephine to hear. She flipped her hair over her shoulder, turned, and followed her sister inside.

The light dazzled the periphery of the black dots. *Go*, the black dots hummed. The glare of the moon shone off a bottle broken on the sidewalk, onto Richmond's car parked at an especially haphazard angle beside the curb in front of Theresa's house.

"The street is black tar slivers," Josephine said out loud as she put the key in the front door. She pretended she was speaking into a tape recorder, recording her observations for posterity, though she was too old now for children. "The light coming from the windows of the house across the street is like an exploded star."

Go, the black dots hummed again, pulsing. Josephine knew what she had to do. She went into the kitchen and cleaned the knife. She traced the outline of her eyes with the sharp edge, imagining the cut at the root that would rid her of the fear. There was a knock on the door.

When Josephine had woken up on the beach that morning, she and her mother were remarkably still under the blanket. She had hoped even then, before things got worse, that they'd be carried out to sea. They went back to the house where her father welcomed them reluctantly back to civilization. He ran his hand across his forehead. This would become his signature gesture, meaning he was tired and couldn't talk to a woman whose possibilities he'd exhausted and the child whom she'd taken as an accomplice.

"Josephine, it's party time," Theresa called through the closed door. Tap, tap. "Ready or not, happiness is coming to get you."

Josephine felt *her* blood flow through *her* veins; *her* heart like a fist pounding on the walls of her chest; *her* breath moving in and out of her lungs. Hers was a different life in a different body. She put the knife back in the drawer and pressed on her closed eyelids with her fingers, tentatively at first and then harder, so she saw spots with her eyes closed. She took her fingers from her eyes and opened them. It was so dark it was as if night had entered the house, and then, slowly, reluctantly, the outline of the world emerged from the black.

THEN how *do* men participate in pregnancy?" Ralph asks. "It's as if the man flies to the place where the kid is born, and the woman takes the train, taking in all the scenery. Pregnancy is like a foreign country she's traveled without him that she'll never be able to explain in full. It'll just sit there between them, untranslatable. The man hovers on the periphery." Ralph can get carried away. He does telemarketing from home to support his painting.

"Oh, Ralph," Rachel, his recently pregnant girlfriend and one of my oldest friends, says. "Enough with the drama. Pass the orange juice."

Both Rachel and Margaret, another old friend of mine, had come to brunch in the cramped one-bedroom Brooklyn apartment where Willie and I live—the rent creeping up and up—each expecting to be the only one with the news. They are both pregnant—Rachel fifteen weeks, Margaret thirteen. All the women at the table have known each other since college; each man since whenever he became involved with whichever woman. We sit around a defective table I got for free from the furniture store where I am a floor hostess. At work I wear skirts that swish and swing. "I am a host-ess," they swish. "I am a host-ess," they swing. My boss, a caster of thick and sturdy shadows, is usually away buying furniture. When he hired me he told me that the way in which I hold myself is an important part of the store atmosphere. "You are a solitary siren," he said. "Luring sailors to our port." I hold firm to the belief that there is a specific kind of dignity in not fighting back.

"He doesn't have to just hover," Willie says suddenly. He's been sitting quietly on the couch, separate from the rest of us, doing what he does best—being quiet but taking everything in, considering.

I met Willie in a car crash four years ago. We weren't going very fast. It wasn't serious. He made a left-hand turn without looking and landed a dent like a giant's punch that still marks the right side of my car. "I'll need your insurance information," he said, realistic from the beginning. He walked toward me carefully, picking his way through glass, though there was very little. He looked studious as he approached me with pen and paper, like someone willing to take notes. "Tell me what I need to know," he said, and I did willingly.

"Well then, tell us, O wise one, what can he do?" Margaret asks.

"Yeah, Willie," Jake, Margaret's husband, says, rubbing his hands together as if he's plotting something. He usually is. "Lay your wisdom on us."

"There are things a man can do," he says mysteriously. He's behaving very suspiciously. He's not looking at me, and suddenly I panic. It's an experience he's had before me? Thinking about getting pregnant again after my miscarriage two years ago has made me extremely paranoid. Willie and I never told anyone about the miscarriage. It happened after eleven weeks—we hadn't even told anyone we were pregnant. It happened so quickly that both of us wondered if it signified something bigger than science, deeper than the statistics that said it happened to one in four women pregnant for the first time. We knew we weren't alone in the experience—we had friends who'd miscarried—but the experience was ours alone.

"What can he do?" I ask pointedly. I give Willie a what-are-you-talking-about look.

"He can educate himself," Willie says. "He can find things out." And then I recognize the tone in his voice—it's the urgent tone he uses when he wants to make a point based on his own experience but he only half-tells because whatever it is he actually experienced is a secret. What he's really saying is that I'm about to find something out, the something that he's half-telling me now. He's giving me that look that says he loves me and we'll talk about all of this later. He's prepping me for something he's been meaning to tell me all along. "He can know the woman so well that he participates alongside her," he says. He looks at me as if this is a promise, and I want to punch him.

This morning just before everyone arrived, I found a picture of Ella with a note from Louise saying hello, asking Willie to say hello to me. Nothing threatening, but there was Ella with a face so like Willie's boyhood face that I'd pointed it out, held it up to Willie. The doorbell rang, and Willie just nodded, holding up a hold-that-thought finger as he walked away from me to answer the door.

Ella is Louise's five-year-old child, and Louise is Willie's ex-girlfriend, *the* girlfriend before me, the one who might have been with Willie now if it hadn't been for a few random incidents. Before I met her, I turned her face into the sweetest porcelain doll in my mind; her hair curly like curly sheep hair; her breasts sweet nectarines. Then I met her, and she was kind, married with a child, and living far, far away, on the other side of the country. Because her husband was infertile, Louise used donated sperm to have Ella, whom I met only that once when she was a toddler. Her round face then was a generic sweet pudge, not the little-girl version of Willie's I saw this morning in the picture.

"Let's make a pact," Jake says suddenly. "We'll all start smoking again when we're seventy."

Margaret turns her back on him and says to Rachel, "Have you been eating food like eating is inevitable, like it's fate? There was a piece of pizza sitting on somebody's desk, somebody I barely know, the other day at work, and I felt drawn to it."

"So what did you do?" Rachel asks.

"I ate it."

It's often on Sundays, the bare day stretched before us, that Willie and I discuss the possibilities. Though I organized the brunch, I was looking forward to after everyone had left, to the quiet afternoon hours alone with Willie when we could remind ourselves of the infinite times decisions like this were made before us—a decision my mother and father made in Georgia or Rhode Island or Colorado, a decision made all across the country as they looked for a permanent home, the right place, the perfect place they never found, until they decided at a certain point that now was as good a time as any, and this place would do as well as anywhere else, and then my mother watched her body grow, fill with a thing alive.

"I'm reading this book," Margaret says. Everyone groans. Margaret is always reading some book that claims to be the definitive whatever. "No, really," she says. "It's one of many, I promise. I'm a multisource woman these days. Pregnancy has changed me."

Jake nods mock-vigorously and Margaret mock-punches him. "I've read that book," Jake says. "There's a ritual called couvade. The man takes to his bed to simulate the delivery of a child as the woman is actually giving birth."

"Oh, great," Rachel says. "I can picture Ralph now—feet up in silk-laced stirrups as nubile young women feed him grapes while somewhere a creepy doctor is prepping me for an episiotomy."

Willie and I have reached that certain point; we are married three years, him with a steady job teaching high school English, me a floor hostess at an imported furniture company. It's not what I'd planned for myself in my mid-thirties, but for now it's fine. Willie and I read a lot; we go to the movies; we take long walks after work. My job has very little to do with my real life.

"I still don't believe either of you is pregnant," Willie says, getting up to get more coffee. "It's too perfect." He raises an eyebrow the way only he can. *"What are you really here to tell us?"*

Now I'm in the mood for a fight. *What if I miscarry again?* turns easily into *What hasn't he told me? Who is this man? How can anyone really know anyone else?* And I'm right back to *How are we ever going to have children if we're total strangers?*

"Okay, okay," Rachel says. "We're really aliens. We want *your* firstborn."

"There must be something in the water," Jake says, holding out his coffee cup for more. "You better look out, Tanya." He squeezes my knee.

Willie looks over and he's smiling that smile again, that smile that tells me we'll talk about all of this later and that he loves me, that we want our firstborn too. But I'm not having any of it. I look away.

"I had a dream we converted our house into a big meat factory," Rachel says. "It was a huge success—people came from all around. It was awkward for other people in the neighborhood. There was tension. Our meat factory wasn't entirely welcome."

"Mmmm," Ralph says, feeding himself a strip of bacon. "Meat."

"Pregnancy dreams are the weirdest—I dreamed last night that I built a huge hand-painted cabinet for Willie and Tanya," Margaret says. "You guys didn't want it—you said it wouldn't fit in your apartment. But it was really clear that even if you did have room you didn't want it."

"It's true, no room at all," I say to Margaret, waving a hand around the apartment but wanting Willie to hear my tone, read into my words. No room for Ella, no room for Louise.

Yesterday at work a woman and a man walked into the store, their bodies jostling each other affectionately. The woman's breasts bounced slightly under her T-shirt as she carried them in on folded arms. The man was tucked safely inside his clothes. They walked as if they knew where they were going, and I curbed the automatic cheek-straining smile my boss insists upon, so as not to intrude. I watched them finger wrought-iron candlesticks and wondered if Willie was thinking of me at that very moment. I realized, not for the first time, that there are countless details in my day that I don't tell Willie. I wished I could transmit all those images that rush through my mind into his mind at the end of the day when I'm too tired to explain; those reels and reels of time when my mind runs wild that he knows nothing about. I wished he could do the same thing for me—the yearnings of our whorish brains captured and transmitted. Sometimes I just stand at the front of the store and yearn for things I can't articulate, and Willie doesn't know anything about it. How can we have a baby if he doesn't know about that yearning? If I can't describe it to him?

"It's just that time of life," Margaret announces, putting her hand over her tea-filled mug as Willie comes toward her with the coffeepot. "The age of having babies. I keep wondering, How did I get old enough for this?"

"I know," Rachel says. "There used to be so much time ahead of us. Pregnancy makes me think of death. Do you think that's bad for the baby?"

"I'll drink coffee for the both of us," Ralph says, ignoring Rachel's question. He holds out his cup.

"I see your pregnancy plane has already taken off, Ralph," Rachel says. Rachel always said she never wanted children and now she's pregnant.

Soon brunch is over. I hurry everyone out. I stop Ralph from doing the dishes. Good-bye. Good-bye. Good-bye. I'm so happy for you. Call me. It's wonderful. So wonderful. It's amazing. Kiss kiss kiss kiss.

Willie and I are left in the profound vacuum of silence that occurs after a group of people leave a room. Willie sits innocently on the floor as if it were a normal Sunday. His legs slide independent of the rest of him through sheaves of the Sunday paper filled with rampant disease in ravaged countries, murder, and the economy. He slides toward me through strewn papers while outside the day's sleepy Sunday glaze that says stay inside and consider life from a distance has become suspect too.

Willie holds my face in his hands and says, "You are so beautiful."

"So? What of it?" I say. "What were you trying to tell me in front of a group of people that you were too scared to tell me in private?"

"What do you mean, *so*? What is that? So." He stalls, sprawling in the swish and crinkle of paper, among the politicians and killers.

"Ella's your child," I say. Just like that, so quickly, but I realize I've been waiting to say this sentence all morning. I ruffle the pages of the book review, clinging to the usual routine, as if everything weren't irrevocably different. There's an ad for a bestseller that Margaret told me she read about a serial killer who keeps the tongues of young women, indistinguishable in pickling jars, on the windowsill in his bathroom. They are blackening specimens, severed from their language.

Willie closes his eyes, and before the rush of everything else that I know I will feel, I am overcome with knowing this man so well that I intuited all of this from a comment he made at brunch to a group of four other people. More than rage, more than anything, this connection makes us not really alone for a moment, makes us as close to each other as we'll ever be.

"Yes," he says cautiously. He's past the moment of connectedness to wondering how he should feel now that he's been found out.

What to do with this information? He donated his sperm to his ex-girlfriend five years ago, before I'd even met him. Why didn't he tell me? Maybe it became one of those reels in his mind that he was too tired to pass on, seemingly unimportant, less and less important as the years went by. What does it even mean? Am I supposed to yell and tear my hair out? Sometimes you just do nothing for a while. Willie stands up, circles around me in order to massage the perpetually tight spot underneath my right shoulder blade, pressing hard to release something deep inside.

"Don't do that," I say.

"I worship you." He gets down on his knees and mock-worships, kissing my bare feet and bowing his head in deference. He puts his arm around me and I feel the warmth of him that over the course of the day, over the course of weeks and months and years, has left and then returns, leaves and returns, leaves and returns. "I want to have a baby with you," he says, his face in my neck.

"Get off me." I shrug him off. I get up and walk toward the sink filled with dishes from the brunch, which seems like years ago now, not sure what to do next. I pick up an apple, consider taking a bite and then drop it. It bounces red against the kitchen floor until it's bruised.

"I'm going out," I say. Willie knows not to come with me. He knows not even to speak. I take the pregnancy book I bought at the used bookstore in our neighborhood with me. I get on the subway and read from an interview with a pregnant woman who talks about sleeping while pregnant. "I am most myself when I am sound asleep," she says. "I wish that I could talk in a dream to my unborn baby."

A young couple not unlike Willie and me sit at the opposite end of the car. They have lots of scrap metal in a bag and a ladder, which they've unfolded so it stands upright in front of them. A man dressed in urine-soaked burlap bags wakes up from a nap at the other end of the car and walks over, considers the ladder, and begins to climb.

My life, this revelation, is not a catastrophe. I know that the secret of Ella will eventually be absorbed into the narrative of our relationship. She will become our secret together, and though there will be tears and we will be changed, we will remain inextricably intertwined.

I get off the subway and walk home, taking my time, in order to cover some terrain without Willie. When I get there, Willie's in bed reading the rest of the paper. I linger between my clothes and my nightgown while Willie watches from the bed. The way he studies me each night like this fills me with significance, but tonight I won't look back.

At work on Friday, there was a tall man wearing loose khaki pants, with broad shoulders, sent by a distributor to set up a display of Macao patio furniture. He carried settees, armchairs, tables, through the front door of the store to the back where the display was, setting them down in an arrangement he thought was best. I watched him move back and forth, smiling at him as if Willie didn't exist, flirting silently until I tripped over my own feet and lurched toward a blue china vase with a tight waist that holds pencils.

There are my own fantasies: all my old lovers in one room. I walk in—surprise!—triumphant, always a little thinner and filled with good news of myself. These men in one room—short and tall, goofy and sophisticated, older and younger, those with whom I might have had a child. But these are just fantasies when I look down at the familiar thick bones of my body, at the veins pushing at the surface of the skin on the inside of my arm, twigs trapped beneath ice.

"That was a stupid way to tell me about Ella," I say, even though *I* told *him.*

"I know," he says. "I was going to tell you years ago, but then the miscarriage . . . It's stupid. I thought you knew, that we had an understanding."

"Out loud," I say, overenunciating. "I need to understand it officially and out loud."

"So now it's official?"

"Don't get so comfortable. This may take a while. I'll need you to explain."

"Well," he begins.

"Not now."

We fall asleep not touching, and I dream that the baby we could have is inside me made of glass. I walk carefully and don't make any sudden moves. I realize I will have to hold still so it can slide out cold and whole. I clear a space on a shelf, move books and a framed picture to make room for the glass baby. I wake up terrified, the antiseptic smell of a hospital in my nostrils.

"It's normal to have dreams like this," Willie says when I wake him up. His head is still on the pillow and he speaks in a whisper though there is no one else to wake up. He's always done this, as if he knew someday it would be necessary.

"I read an interview in that pregnancy book," Willie says hopefully, now that he's got my attention back. "A woman told the interviewer that she felt a strong beam of love. 'I felt as if I were shining my light on the relationship with my husband,' she said."

I imagine her flashing her high beams on her husband, caught unaware on the road. "A few chapters later," I say, "she tells her that she never imagined she could feel so sick."

"Great," he says. I fit myself reluctantly into Willie's outstretched arms, putting my head on his chest the way we always do at the beginning of the night though we will end up on opposite sides of the bed by morning.

I remember waving out the window as a child from a babysitter's arms as my parents left in a swirl of soap and perfume for a party. I forgot them while they were gone and thrilled at their return. It is that animalistic thrill that is my initial desire. That someone that small would smell the air instinctively for my scent, and thrill at my return. There are pictures of Willie as a child where he is stiff with that kind of excitement and anticipation.

But there is something before that, before the actual baby. There are Willie's genes and my genes meeting inside of me, beginning a conversation apart from either of us. Like ambassadors from foreign countries sent to negotiate, through a mixture of cocktail banter and lofty ideas they will come to some kind of agreement. I imagine that years from now the interviewer asks me whether I dreamed about my unborn baby. "The baby was never in my dreams," I'll say to her. "The baby was in my body dreaming with me, dreaming the language of my body." The last time the conversation had only just begun. For that dreamy conversation, there is this part of me that is willing.

I look up at Willie's face. His eyes are open—small, shiny plates in the dark. He will not go to sleep on me. We will stay up all night in these separate bodies.

THE ARRANGEMENT OF THE
NIGHT OFFICE IN SUMMER

Contemplation

The midnight moon sheds solemn light on the low wooden fences that mark the boundaries of my parents' neighborhood. I step easily over as I take my usual late-night walk, passing through newly mown lawns littered with the junk of leisurely East Coast summer lives—thick, abandoned paperbacks, their pages warped from reading by the pool; one flip-flop lost from its pair; still-damp towels hung over the handlebars of children's bikes to dry.

Every night a different route, and tonight I stumble over a tribe of naked Barbies, their pointed feet jammed into the earth. They stand menacing and alert in a series of semicircles, like the guests (only naked) waiting for my younger sister's fourth wedding to begin two days ago. Beyond the Barbie tribe, the yard swims with the remains of an afternoon spent lounging in the thick humidity—an empty pitcher; two tumblers, rims laced with salt. I trip over a sprinkler and lie still in the soft, cool grass, straining to listen to the world through the ear of my heart, the way Elliot, the professor I do research for in a university town in the Midwest, has encouraged me to do.

On the airplane ride here, in the plane with twenty seats, the stewardess smiled and announced, "Your closest exit may be behind you." One of Saint Benedict's edicts lodged itself in my mind: *Day by day, remind yourself that you are going to die.* I took a couple of Ativan instead, and as the plane took off I chanted under my breath. "Flying is boring. Flying is boring," as the plane shimmied and shook down the runway, finally heaving itself into the air.

The Ativan had just begun its work on the muscle level—small twitches in my cheeks and hands—when the woman next to me mistook my involuntary movement for an invitation to converse.

"I'm a writer. What do you do?" she said.

The plane dipped ominously. Flying is boring. Flying is boring. "Well," I said. I didn't feel like explaining my status as eternal grad student, suspended in time like a perfect fruit fly in amber, or fluffing up my job as assistant researcher on a book about Benedictine monks. "I'm a librarian."

I could have lied in any direction. Her question was a decoy, bobbing politely on the surface of our conversation, useless and hollow. She began her monologue.

"It was a sudden decision for me, really. A quick realization," she said. "One day God slapped me on the ass and told me to be a writer." What I had initially interpreted as hip funkiness—chunky turquoise earrings, wild salt-and-pepper hair, bright red lipstick—began to look more and more like the signs of a woman with questionable boundaries.

"I had no other choice," she said. "Absolutely, no other choice. I've given up reading altogether. Not even the newspaper. I realized finally that it would corrupt the purity of my writing process."

"I'm going to my younger sister's wedding." I held it up like a shield.

"I remember when my sisters got married. I'm one of five, you know," the woman said. "Nine weddings, all divorced now. We weren't cut out for commitment." When she spoke, her earrings rattled.

When the plane shuddered and the engine's deafening roar became a suspicious grumble, I headed for the bathroom. Pushing through my Ativan haze up the aisle, I had a vision of my underwear—crumpled and lying in years of unswept office dust, hair, and fingernail clippings—underneath Elliot's desk where he'd pushed it with the toe of his shoe when a student began knocking on his office door. It made me wonder if there is an age when life is supposed to take off like a plane, when something as big as takeoff is supposed to happen.

A screen door slams, and a big hairy dog skids across the porch, toenails clattering. He bounds toward the nearest tree, lifts his leg to take a leak. When he's done, he licks the salt off the tumblers and trots over to where I lie. He sniffs at my shoes, then snuffles his way up the rest of my body. With his margarita tongue, he licks away the tears rolling down the side of my face, then walks in those mysterious doggie circles, lies down with his head on my stomach, and falls asleep.

Y ou stink like dog," my sister Lanie says, eyes still closed, when I climb in next to her in her childhood bed. We've been sharing it since her fiancé, Jack, disappeared three days ago, the day before they were supposed to be married in my parents' backyard. We are surrounded by dusty furniture moved "temporarily" from other rooms, stacks of yellowing magazines, and a papier-mâché clown head that Lanie made in high school. It lurks in the corner, a shadowy monster.

"Ruff, ruff," I say, licking her cheek.

"That," she says, wiping her face with the sheet, "is disgusting." I watch her settle back into sleep. She heaves a few deep sighs and fades gently into herself. In there, swirling and colliding, are dreams she'll tell me about tomorrow. She is capable of the perfect dream, or at least of *composing* the perfect dream, the one that resolves the problems of today, integrating all the necessary players. Today she told me last night's dream of Jack gambling away her life savings in Atlantic City, where he is in reality holding the hand of an ex-girlfriend as she dies of AIDS, alone in a dirty apartment she can no longer afford. In Lanie's dream, Jack rolled her wedding ring like dice across the green felt of a craps table.

Each night I roam the neighborhood and then lie in bed listening to what's left of the waiting family breathe. My mother and father in their bed; Aunt Bernadette in my old room, smelling of new car upholstery and the cigarillos she smokes since she quit smoking cigarettes; cousin George and his new girlfriend whom no one likes, on the foldout couch in the living room. Carl, Lanie's second husband, and Kevin, his boyfriend, in the guest room. As a group, we possess the qualities of a freshman college hall mixed with those of the only remaining survivors of a made-for-TV-movie nuclear holocaust—we eat whatever's in the house and stay indoors, paralyzed by catastrophe but secretly happy for an excuse not to do our homework.

"We're staying," Carl declared when it became clear that Jack wasn't showing up for the ceremony. Over the years Carl has remained one of Lanie's closest friends. He called someone at the community college where he works to substitute for the English comp classes he hates teaching anyway. "I'm not going anywhere," Aunt Bernadette said, taking a long drag of her cigarillo. She would manage her real estate business from here, no problem. "We won't leave you in your time of need," George's girlfriend, Lizzie, said. No one had figured out precisely what it was that Lizzie did for a living, and even now, three days later, all we know is that it has to do with marketing something to someone. Lanie looked at me and mouthed, "Who *is* she?"

"Please, everyone stay," my mother said, pushing my father and his scowl aside. My parents have recently reconciled after a six-month separation during which my father lived next door. She turns and looks at my father. "Lanie needs us." Kevin was already on the phone to the airline, agreeing to pay a seventy-five-dollar service charge in order to change his and Carl's return flight. "I'll call the rental car place," George assured Lizzie, who whispered her concerns in his ear. George's business partner would handle the bulk of their web design business from New York. "It's the internet," George assured Lanie when she protested. "The internet is everywhere."

Lanie shifts, resting her cheek on my shoulder. She flings an arm around my waist, demanding my attention in her sleep. "That's ridiculous," she says to someone in the mysterious land of her dream mind.

Suddenly, I want to wake her up and tell her everything I haven't told her over the past several years—how my arrangement with Elliot, which at first had seemed like an ideal substitute for a boyfriend or a religion, has become bizarre and slightly frightening; how I suspect I've become a full-fledged atheist, unable to believe in the god of marriage or the god of career, never mind the regular god; how there are nights I lie awake in my apartment, staring out the window at the lonely night sky so big and vast and me so small and afraid; how I wonder how to feel less separate from the world around me, then wonder how it's possible that I've wondered the exact same thing year after year lying in different beds looking at different patches of sky. But instead I look at Lanie's hand draped over my hip, filled with energetic purpose even in sleep.

I miss her already. We will all have to return to our lives at some point, which leads me, as most things do in the middle of the night, to death. I convince myself that I can stand the thought of my own death more than I can bear Lanie's death someday, her bones crumbling to dust. I begin to weep—at first from the inside out and then it's just my body going through the motions, practicing, working out for death as if one could be in shape for it, ready to run its marathon when it finally arrives.

Community

"Harriet," Aunt Bernadette says to me, pausing to light a cigarillo at the breakfast table where we're all drinking mimosas meant for the wedding brunch. Lanie has cut the heads off of the flowers in her wedding bouquet—roses, delphiniums, hollyhocks, dahlias—and floated them in a bowl of water at the center of the table. They bob brilliant red and yellow and blue. It's just like Lanie to make something extraordinary out of disaster, orchestrating her own abandonment like a party.

"It's ten o'clock in the morning, Bernadette," my mother says to her sister, waving her hand through the exhaled smoke.

"Lay off. You have Sam, I have these." Bernadette pats the pack in the pocket of her bathrobe. "Anyway, look who's talking, Ms. I'm-working-on-my-third-mimosa. Don't pretend to be a priss. It doesn't suit you."

"Sam is not a pack of cigarettes," my mother says. Her voice is shrill with the twenty years of tension that run like currents of electricity underneath the surface of this exchange.

"I'll get the banana bread." My father heads for the kitchen.

"Perfect," Lanie says, her voice pure and resonant as the oboe she played in the high school band. She speaks without lifting her head from the table as Carl massages her neck and shoulders.

"That doesn't bother you?" Lizzie, George's girlfriend, says to Kevin, Carl's boyfriend, sitting next to her.

"No, does it bother *you*?" Kevin has no patience with Lizzie since the night of the ceremony that didn't happen. After polishing off a bottle of wine by herself, Lizzie started telling drinking stories from her sorority days. When it became clear that no one wanted to hear about the time she took a shit on a sorority sister's bed that she mistook for a toilet, she cornered Kevin and began asking him questions about his sex life. *Doesn't it hurt? Is Carl's penis bigger or smaller than yours? Don't you ever miss girls? Not even a little?* At which point George peeled her off of Kevin and led her upstairs to the bathroom. "Just so long as she doesn't take a dump on *my* bed," Lanie whispered to me.

"It would bother *me*," Lizzie says now.

"Guess what, Lizzie? Kevin *isn't* you," George says. He's lost patience with her too.

"I was just asking."

"Harriet," Bernadette says again. Again, she pauses, lighting a new cigarillo.

"For Christ's sake, what?" I was hoping she'd been distracted. I can feel her urge to ally herself with me from across the table—just a couple of single girls holding out for a love that will transform us. The trouble is I'm not holding out, and I don't want to be on her team. My mother doesn't want me on Bernadette's team either.

For the most part, my mother chooses to see my life as faraway, something she can't quite make out in the distance, but then she panics and sends me negligees and hair combs, the bait with which to lure a man. She imagines that if I stand at my bedroom window with my hair pulled back and my negligee arranged just so, men will swarm to me like worker bees to a queen. "Don't end up like Bernadette," my mother told me over the phone last week. "Finding love and staying in love are acts of will. Look at me and your father. Sheer will and determination." For her, love is like exercise—something you endure in order to feel virtuous.

"Nice mouth for a girl who studies monks," Carl says to me now, working a knot under Lanie's right shoulder blade.

"Is that what you're doing in Illinois?" Bernadette says. "Working with monks?"

"Yes," I say. "I fuck them too."

"Jesus, Harriet," Lanie says. She gives me a look that tells me not to contribute to the chaos.

"You'd think you two actually had a personal relationship with the man given the number of times you've called on Jesus in the past minute," Bernadette says. She blows smoke in my mother's direction.

"Don't give us that holier-than-thou crap, Ms. I-go-once-every-six-months-to-Quaker-meeting. It's not like we never mentioned him while the girls were growing up. *Jesus fucking Christ.*" My mother laughs, and Bernadette's smoking is forgiven, as is her age-old critique of what Bernadette sees as my mother's inability to live without my father. Bernadette thinks my mother has settled for something less than spectacular, though Bernadette lives miserably alone, unable to settle for anything.

"So," Bernadette says, "you're fucking monks in Illinois?"

"Is there any hope for a little dignity and decorum at the breakfast table?" my mother asks. "Some of us actually believe in God around here."

"You do?" George asks.

"Don't you?" Lizzie says, turning to George.

"How can you even know?" says Carl. "I mean, why beat yourself up trying to know?"

"What I really think we should all be asking ourselves,"

Kevin says in the voice of a recent presidential candidate, "is *What would Jesus do?* What would Jesus do if Jack hadn't called *him* since standing him up at the altar?"

The room falls silent. Everyone looks to Lanie for guidance. She laughs but it sounds like a cough.

"I'm laughing," she says. "I'm *laughing*."

Carl stops kneading Lanie's shoulder to punch Kevin on the arm.

"Ow," says Kevin.

"I admit it," my mother says, in an effort to keep things from disintegrating entirely. "I believe in God."

"What do you want? A medal?" Bernadette says.

"I'm just saying." My mother gets up from the table and heads for the kitchen.

"Can I have one of those nasty things?" Lanie holds out her hand to Bernadette for a cigarillo.

"Me too," says Lizzie, in an effort to befriend Lanie.

"Clearly, the massage isn't working." Carl throws up his hands and returns to his seat beside Kevin. He rests his forehead dramatically on Kevin's shoulder. "I'm a failure."

"No, you're not," Lanie says. "I just need some chemical backup."

"More mimosas?" my mother calls from the kitchen.

Everyone groans.

"You have no choice when it comes to this banana bread." My father waltzes in with a steaming plate held high above his head.

"He cooks, he cleans, he's superman!" Bernadette puts her

most recent cigarillo out with a hiss in the swallow of liquid at the bottom of her champagne glass.

But we're all watching Lanie. She holds the cigarillo in one hand and procures the perfect bite of banana bread with the other. We are, all of us, rapt—Carl, Kevin, my mother, my father, George, who used to pine for her until it was explained to him at thirteen that it wasn't appropriate to French-kiss your first cousin. Even Lizzie puts aside her confusion and jealousy, because Lanie has that kind of power over people. She is a magnetic force, especially in her grief over Jack. The way she inhales smoke with her eyes closed gives us all intense pleasure, and the way she licks the crumbs from her fingers sends us all reaching for a piece of the banana bread, though eating it will never taste as good as watching Lanie. She steals an ice cube from George's water glass and runs it along her collarbone, heated up from inside her long body. She rubs the dripping water into her skin as if it were lotion.

Even as a girl, she gave off an electric glow—eating ice cream in the morning, though my parents told her not to, would somehow end up being funny. The same is true of all of her marriages. She says each of them has been like school— her first one like high school—basic and tragic; Carl was like college—almost grown-up and life-altering; her third like graduate school—overly analytic; and now there's Jack. Jack, she told us, is like being sent back to junior high, being forced to wear braces and have acne all over again.

Bernadette breaks the spell. "Harriet," she says. She's determined to put her pain somewhere else. She's had a bad year of younger men who broke her heart, first with their yearning for her and then with that sudden, fickle indifference specific to men of a certain age who haven't yet realized their power and then suddenly, brutally do. "Harriet, have you met any strapping, cornfed, midwestern men?"

Lizzie rises from her slump next to George, eager to earn Kevin's forgiveness for the other night. "Why do you assume it's a man?" She looks to Kevin, but he is focused intensely on his banana bread.

George goes red and takes his plate into the kitchen, which has become the designated safe zone. He runs water, pretends to wash dishes.

"No cornfed strappers—man, woman, or beast," I say.

Lanie comes to my rescue. She takes my hand, pulling me up from my seat as if she were asking me to dance. "Enough of this silliness," she announces. "These sisters are going upstairs."

Restraint of Speech

There are times when silence is better, even, than good words. Saint Benedict discovered this when he renounced his world in the sixth century—the Roman empire disintegrating all around him, emperors being deposed in the midst of constant war. He went to live in a cave thirty miles east of Rome, in search of structure, security, and stability.

"Silence works to counteract our culture of anxiety,"

Elliot told me. The snow that first winter in Illinois seemed to fall constantly, rendering the world, our world inside his office, doubly silent.

It happened the first time as if by accident, but looking back I see there was nothing accidental about it, that in fact it grew organically out of studying people whose lives were efforts at controlled meditation. Halfway into it, I took a step in his direction, on the brink, moving toward him not because I wanted to but because I thought that was the right thing to do; the instinct to share that blast of pleasure seemed appropriate after the slow, teasing seduction of watching each other remove our own clothes, watching each other's hands as they moved down to begin their steady, rhythmic work.

But Elliot stopped me. "Stay there," he said softly from where he stood on the other side of his desk, naked, his hand moving in swift measured strokes.

Soon the routine became clear—when I arrived, the day would be circled on the hanging calendar made by the Benedictine brotherhood of Saint John's, each month a spare pencil drawing depicting scenes with titles like *The Good Zeal of Monks, Brothers on a Short Journey,* or *The Times for the Brothers' Meals.* The day circled was never fixed, but once a week, there it would be. The first day, the scene depicted was *The Sleeping Arrangements of the Monks.* I've learned to look without *looking* as if I'm looking—a quick, imperceptible turn of my head as I walk through Elliot's office door. Will we retreat to the cave today? Yes, I take my place, my body already a dull purr, readying itself for the steady hum. No, we hit the books, turning away from our desires, plunging instead into the comprehension of these strange men who sometimes sleep in their clothes so they can be ready to serve God immediately upon rising.

Most people assume monks are celibate, that they've rung out the last vestiges of sexual want drop by drop. But it is possible for monks to integrate a new, refigured sexuality into a constant dialogue with common love and monastic celibacy. There is instead an intensification, a heightening, a focus. One learns to draw the lines, to avoid foolish chatter lest one slip and slide in a flood of words.

We do not touch. We do not speak. We never speak. We make no noise, no sounds, no moans or squeals. We do not say each other's names. In this way I've convinced myself that there is room for something else, some altered consciousness between us standing as we do, leaning against opposite walls for support. There are moments when I feel an invisible presence in the room with us, a wind in the sealed office blowing through me, the moment rising up out of our combined efforts, to skim my soul. We limit our movements. We move our hands just enough. We wait for each other, slowing down to let the other catch up, always monitoring the pace, and when the time comes, we turn away. Though we have never articulated any of the terms of our arrangement, there is an unspoken agreement that we will not look, that the final moment is each of ours to have privately.

Just once, I caught Elliot looking at me as he came into the trashcan lined with a plastic bag. "I am truly a worm, not a man," he said when he saw that I'd seen him looking. And for days afterward, I turned his words over in my mind—did he mean to begin a conversation? was it a conversation I wanted to be a part of? hadn't I achieved a celibacy of my own? would I sacrifice that? I spent long nights, tiny in my bed, staring out my window at the vast sky wondering what Elliot might offer me in the way of comfort, allowing myself to imagine the unwashed, sleepy skin-smell of it, the sound of my name in his mouth surrounded by tenderness, the salty ocean taste of him. The words began to seem, after twisting and turning them, strangely familiar. A week later, I came across the line—*I am truly a worm, not a man*—in *The Rule of Saint Benedict*, a recommendation, a mantra for life.

Obedience

Downstairs, I hear my father's voice straining to be heard— "Americans have faith in faith"—as, midsentence, my mother begins to slide the vacuum cleaner around the room, sucking up the crumbs under the legs of the breakfast table.

"For Christ's sake," my father shouts over the sound.

"Here we go again with Christ. Poor guy," Bernadette says, as my mother turns off the vacuum.

"I didn't realize we were having a serious conversation anymore," my mother says.

"Sit down next to me," George says. My mother is his favorite aunt. "Sit here, and talk to me."

In Lanie's old room, dusty sunlight comes through the windows in patterns that slice Lanie into various rectangular sections where she lounges on the bed. I sit on a coffee table that used to be downstairs in the living room, now relegated to Lanie's room because of concentric circular wood scars made by glasses left too long without coasters.

"How are you?" I ask Lanie.

"You know, I'm fine," she says, looking out the window, over the lawn statues and the yard next door with the cherub fountain spitting that sounds like rain. "Really fine." She looks out past the yards, beyond our lives, to the horizon.

"Have you heard from Jack?"

She falls back on the bed and walks her socked feet up the wall. "Let's not talk about that. Tell me something about you."

"Well," I say. "I'm not sure what to tell you. I seem to be in a holding pattern. I'm waiting for something to slice the blurry edges off my life, to reveal itself, but I'm not sure what that something is."

"That's it," she says, sitting up attentively as the conversation turns away from her. "That's exactly it, Harriet. You postpone pleasure. Look at us here right now. I'm as comfortable as I can possibly be. I'm lying on the bed, and you're sitting on the edge of a stained, cast-off table. What are you holding out for? You wait, and I luxuriate. You've got to work with what you've got."

"But you're waiting for Jack." I throw it back at her. She knows nothing about the facts of my life, but she's intu-

ited something at its core and it makes me want to humili-
ate her.

"Yes, but he's *something*," she says. "You don't even know
what you're waiting for."

"I wish my life were that easily defined," I snap.

"I'm sorry," Lanie says, her voice, that sacred instrument,
full of regret. "Yesterday, Jack said he'd call this morning and
he hasn't. This woman, his ex-girlfriend, is almost dead. He's
sitting there in the room with her all day. She can barely
whisper, she's hallucinating. He's hired a live-in nurse, but
he's staying to keep her company so that she doesn't have to
die with a stranger. I don't *want* her to die alone. I don't want
that, but I'm jealous of her with him there, watching over
her. I hate him. I hate myself. I want him to call me and tell
me she's dead, that she's vanished from the earth forever and
ever. But when she dies, it'll be worse. He never got over her,
and when she dies he never will. There's always that one per-
son who fucks you up for life, and he's going to be mine." She
flips over and squirms across the bed toward me, holds out
her hand. "I'm sorry. I'm awful when I'm not married." I take
her hand in both of mine.

"I want to show you something I found."

I rummage through my bag to retrieve the photograph I
stole back from Elliot's office. It's worn and faded as if rubbed
by fingers longing to go back to that time. Black-robed fig-
ures mill around snowy stone buildings in a cold, long-ago
place. I first found the picture stuck between the pages of a
library book. I held it by one edge as I drove as fast as the

stoplights would allow, from my apartment to Elliot at the state university, one of the old Normal schools for teachers where people specialize in facts tiny and hard as ring-size gems. I drove the picture carefully past the false fronts on the brick buildings of Main Street, the few high-rise student dorms stabbing their way into the sky, the rumpled, tree-filled blocks of relaxed midwestern prosperity, heading for Elliot's office dedicated to the celebration of small things. He couldn't speak when I gave it to him. He just stood there, his academic awards hanging behind him with his name spelled out in solid strokes of calligraphy suggesting an indelible community. "For that long," he said, his whisper rustling through his beard, "they've been asking each other: How many of us are in vows out of fear rather than love?"

"They date back to fifth-century Rome," I tell Lanie.

"When was this picture taken?"

"I'm not sure," I say. "Elliot thinks it was taken around the turn of the century."

"Is Elliot the history professor you work for?" Work is a foreign language that Lanie doesn't speak. When her first husband died he left her money enough to pursue her curiosities with casual abandon, curiosities that have ranged from performance art to day trading.

"Yes."

"Do you love him?" She looks up from the picture. If I did, we would have that in common, loving someone who doesn't love us back.

"No," I say, fairly certain that it's not him that I love, that what I love is that invisible presence that lies between us. "No, I don't love him."

Lanie and I look back at the monks overcoming the worldly concerns of a life that seems too small, walking the fields searching for a god or anyone to receive the ceremony of their beliefs.

As Lanie rubs her eye with the back of her hand like a little sister and not a wife for the fourth time, I wonder what all this tying and untying the knot means to her. I wonder what the knot is exactly. I want to know whether marriage for Lanie means safety like a crash helmet or whether it is some sweeter form of security, but I can't ask these questions because Lanie and I don't talk this way about her life. I want to tell her that I'm not so much yearning for men as I am yearning for something like what Lanie sees in men, a confirmation of life, a sign that all is well.

Voices from downstairs erupt through the silence between us.

"He's not coming back," Carl says. "I always told her he was a selfish asshole."

"Quiet," George says.

"Stay," my mother says. "All of you. Stay here, just a little longer."

"Jesus H. Christ," Bernadette exclaims. "Christ on the cross. Jesus, Mary, and Joseph."

"Stop it," Lizzie says. "It's not funny anymore."

"She's right," Lanie says. "It's really not funny."

• • •

We spend the day in our pajamas. We finish off the mimosas. Tipsy, we wander the house as if its carpeted rooms were all there was to the world. We escape into books, music, the newspaper, draping ourselves across couches, hugging pillows, while Bernadette chain-smokes her cigarillos. At one point Lanie grabs a pillow, inhaling deeply from our childhood, and does a little dance with it. Even my father laughs. When the mimosas begin to wear off, everyone naps. Lanie and I lie down at the foot of George and Lizzie's pull-out sofa bed to sleep. Lanie's stomach is my pillow, the soft carpet our bed. I wake up first and peer through a window at my father standing in the driveway as he pulls the cuff of a pant leg up to scratch at his ankle with garden shears. Our mother sits on the edge of the boxed hedges with her head in her hands, talking but not for anyone else to hear.

Humility

Lanie jerks in her sleep and says words that punch the night. I stroke her hair until she stops moving. When I was a I child, I thought I would be a different person when I grew up. My hair would not be so stringy, it would be thick and lush and long, and I'd pile it on top of my head in elaborate knots stuck through with pencils and paintbrushes. My skin would go from sunburn pale to a dusky olive hue with mysterious, serious shadows. I would be thin-boned and tall and think thoughts that had never occurred to me before. I'd wake up one day, having memorized passages from important books, with fully formulated, important opinions that stopped people in their tracks. I would always, always finish my sentences. Transformed through a mysterious ritual, my life would be utterly different. There would be something now to show me that I was more than just bigger. But here, in the middle of the night, with Lanie talking in her sleep—*Stop going so fast. You're going too fast*—life is endless unmarked territory.

The door to my parents' room is the tiniest bit ajar, and through the crack I glimpse my mother pressed against my father's back, as if she were resting against a wall. In my old room, the door swung wide open, Aunt Bernadette sprawls on her back wheezing her cigarillo breath. I lean against the guest room door to listen to Carl and Kevin's hushed tones rise and fall in the secret language of couples. Downstairs, Lizzie and George are tangled in each other's arms, achieving a depth of comfort that eludes them in waking life. I am suddenly and terribly alone. *Death is boring. Death is boring. Death is boring.*

Out on the back patio, I wait for my eyes to adjust. *Death is boring. Death is boring.* In the eerie blue of night, the yards seem full of hidden treasure sunk to the bottom of an ocean. The whole neighborhood is submerged in the watery glow of the moon, like Lanie's dream the first night we were here—my family swimming through our house filled with water, everyone breathing effortlessly, and finally no talking. A dog barks anonymously from the dark corner of a house but stops once I find the shadows again. I watch for sprinklers lurking in the grass, picking my way through yards as if across minefields.

The Barbie tribe has been pillaged—Barbies everywhere, knocked over and legs splayed. Some of them have choppy, dull-knife haircuts and lipstick smears on their tiny faces. *Death is boring. Death is boring.*

The spitting cherub fountain says I'm almost home. I step over the knee-high stone wall—an unusual variation on the typical faux-wood fence—that separates the house two doors down from the Wallenborns, the family next door who took my father in during my parents' separation. *Death is boring. Death is boring.* The lights in their house are out and the house itself seems to be sleeping. The moon reflects off the shallow fountain pool underneath the cherub spitting. I put my face into the cold water so inviting, a relief from the hot summer. I listen to the blood rush through my head. The second time I do it, I'm looking for a different kind of relief. *Death is boring. Death is boring.* Evolution, natural selection, transcendence, whatever has led me to this moment, I let my head fall like a stone, dipped in the silent splendor of the cold, cold water, not breathing effortlessly, not breathing at all, wanting to feel what it's like just for a moment to not breathe, to not think, to be that quiet.

I get a noseful of water and come up sputtering and chok-

ing. The yard is flooded with sudden light. The Wallenborns'
house has woken up all at once, each window awash in fluo-
rescent yellow.

"There, over there," Mr. Wallenborn screams.

I spew water.

"Don't move. Put your hands up. Get down on the
ground."

"Honey," Mrs. Wallenborn says, squeezing her husband's
shoulder, "it's Harriet."

Mr. Wallenborn shines his flashlight onto my dripping
face. I hiccup and water dribbles out the side of my mouth.
Mr. and Mrs. Wallenborn's faces are frozen in shock to learn
that something so familiar could disturb their night.

"Aren't you in Illinois, Harriet?" Mrs. Wallenborn asks.

My mother, my father, Aunt Bernadette, Carl, Kevin,
George, and Lizzie are standing on the front steps of my par-
ents' house as Mr. Wallenborn escorts me, his hand on my
elbow as if he were escorting me down the aisle. Huge moths
click their wings against the front porch light as my mother
pulls her sweater closed over her nightgown, though there is
no chill in the air.

"She must have been sleepwalking," Mr. Wallenborn says.

"Did she sleepwalk into a pool?" Kevin asks. "Go get a
blanket or something," he says to Carl.

"Why don't you get a blanket if you know so much?" Carl
says affectionately.

"I'll get one," Lizzie says. She turns to George. "Where do I get a blanket?"

"I'll come with you," George says. He is only half awake, and the spell of their sleeping clinch lingers.

"Next time, you might find yourself wandering down the middle of a busy street." Mr. Wallenborn looks at my parents knowingly.

"Come inside," my mother says, when she finds her voice. "Let's go inside. I'll make some coffee."

"In the middle of the night?" Bernadette asks.

"Decaf," my mother says, so confused she doesn't notice that Bernadette is mocking her.

"Thank you, Joe." My father shakes Mr. Wallenborn's hand solemnly—for bringing his daughter safely home, for the time he spent sleeping on his couch, for living day after day in the house next door.

W e gather around the dining room table in our pajamas, including Mr. Wallenborn, who, after politely standing for several minutes to take a few requisite sips of coffee, excuses himself.

"I don't want Jean to worry," he says.

"Of course not," my mother says, guiding him to the door with a grateful hand on his shoulder. "Thank you," she says solemnly, as if he had saved my life.

"You might want to strap her in tonight." He nods toward me and then winks at my mother.

"We'll do that," she says.

Bernadette mimes putting on a seat belt. "Click," she says. For now, everyone is willing to believe I was sleepwalking, though when I sleep, I'm the stillest sleeper in the family.

Lizzie comes in and wraps a blanket around me, though I'm practically dry and it's unbearably hot.

"Well," George says.

"I've got to go back to sleep," Carl says. "I'm exhausted." He stands to take his coffee cup into the kitchen.

"Right," my father says.

Just then Lanie comes down the stairs, her nightgown fluttering around her.

"Where were you?" she asks me, but doesn't stop moving for an answer. She walks out the front door, lifting her arms like wings as she walks down the front steps in a way that says she will banish Jack. She floats lightly, bouncing on bare toes.

We follow her out, riveted, waiting for her to tell us what to do next. She spins at the end of the driveway, a ghostly twirl in the night.

"It's time we all went home," she says. Watch this small thing, says the arch of each of her feet stepping; watch this because it means everything. This foot making gentle contact with the earth, this is how we will survive.

⚑ Perennial

Books by Maud Casey:

DRASTIC: *Stories*
ISBN 0-06-051255-5 (paperback)

In this stunning collection of powerful and piercing stories, Maud Casey explores how we survive modern crises of loss and love. Her characters, emotional and geographic nomads, are haunted by loneliness. Though they flirt with madness and self-destruction, Casey's characters reach toward life.

"A primer on the genealogy of loneliness. . . . Minimalist. . . . Well-written. . . . Its theme of loss made palpable and powerful."
—*New York Times Book Review*

THE SHAPE OF THINGS TO COME: *A Novel*
ISBN 0-06-008441-3 (paperback)
A *NEW YORK TIMES* NOTABLE BOOK

Insightful and entertaining, this gracefully written novel depicts the comedy of being a grown-up still coming of age. Through the hilarious foibles and moving revelations of our 30-something heroine Isabelle, Maud Casey beautifully and evocatively reveals how people narrate their lives to counter the chaotic randomness of modern existence.

"Casey is a stand-up philosopher posing the most vexing questions about human existence. . . . She's funny and inventive . . . [taking] a dazzling narrative dare."
—*New York Times Book Review*